Anne Peile was born in London; she has lived in the South-west and Belfast and has worked as a cook, writing emails for the BBC and in educational support. She lives on a houseboat and works for Foyle's bookstores.

Repeat it today with tears

Anne Peile

A complete catalogue record for this book can
be obtained from the British Library on request

The right of Anne Peile to be identified as the author of this work
has been asserted by her in accordance with the Copyright, Designs
and Patents Act 1988

First published in 2010 by Serpent's Tail,
an imprint of Profile Books Ltd
3A Exmouth House
Pine Street
London EC1R 0JH
website: www.serpentstail.com

ISBN 978 1 84668 746 4

Designed and typeset by sue@lambledesign.demon.co.uk
Printed and bound in Great Britain by Clays, Bungay, Suffolk

10 9 8 7 6 5 4 3 2 1

Mixed Sources
Product group from well-managed
forests and other controlled sources
www.fsc.org Cert no. TT-COC-002227
© 1996 Forest Stewardship Council
FSC

I'm Tad

For my father

PART ONE

The first time I kissed my father on the mouth it was the Easter holiday. A chill clear spring afternoon, the trees still black twigs and a lemon glaze on the white cloud sky. The room looked down upon Phene Street, a small quiet road in Chelsea.

Through the window I had been watching the dog from the Phene Arms, overweight as pub dogs tend to be, rummaging in a garden hedge. Sensing that I was so close to joy, even the heedless dog seemed a toy, a comedic charm staged expressly for my amusement. I watched it for a moment longer, and then I stepped forward and kissed my father on his lovely mouth.

It was a wide mouth but the lips themselves, beneath the modelled philtrum, were thin and pressed, especially so the top one, as if he were frequently angry or displeased or feeling pain. Perhaps because he had once drunk heavily but nowadays did not.

The kiss was of such bliss that even in the moment of its ending, as there was only air between us again, I had acknowledged and accepted that I could never have another like it. I could say that it was an attar of kisses, worth taking even just for once in a life. The Devil is not ungenerous when he makes you a bargain.

My father merely turned away and said, 'Oh, Christ.' In other

circumstances a thought might have flitted across my mind, a
spindly stick of anxiety that he had not liked my kiss and that
was why he had said, 'Oh, Christ.' It did not though; in none of
this did I ever know any doubt.

His back towards me, he stood in front of the painting desk,
his long rangy body and the shoulders slightly stooped. On the
desk were laid out the inks for an illustration he was finishing;
it was a vignette of a landscape with hills, a commission for the
Radio Times.

In my head there was a self-sufficient triumph, a very quiet
and sure triumph for one who was not yet seventeen.

'I'll go now,' I said, to the length of his penitent's back and his
bowed, ashamed head. His hair was falling forwards, it was the
colour of unpolished brass. I could see that his fingers with their
beautiful half-moon cuticles – which I had not inherited – were
pressed upon the edge of the desk.

'See you then,' I said. I closed the door as on a sleeping person
and walked down the three flights of stairs from the room in
Oakley Street and felt that I was filled with grace.

I should explain our history, until that day in Chelsea in 1972.
Mine more so, because he was only there at the beginning and
at the end.

My father, Jack, John ap Rhys Owen, was born in South Wales
in 1916. His father was a mining engineer; the family owned the
town colliery and much of the town itself. They were wealthy
and comfortable although his mother mourned in perpetuity for
the daughter named Ora who had died. My father was indulged
and a ne'er-do-well in youth. Discreetly expelled from Clifton
College, he dallied with this pursuit and that, never settling to
anything, spending freely, and drinking heavily.

In the late 1930s, the health of both parents in decline, the family left Wales for ever and moved to a mansion flat in Finchley Road. My father, contrite and remorseful in his hangovers, would buy his mother little boxes of coloured Kunzle cakes to tempt her to eat. Perhaps also to please her, he announced his engagement to one of the girls from the crowd with whom he went to jazz clubs and to Skindles on Monkey Island and for weekends at Brooklands racing circuit. She was small and blonde, I believe. They married in August 1939 and my father joined the Navy on the day that war broke out. During the war his parents died, within weeks of each other. He, serving on the Arctic convoys, was unable to attend either bedside or funeral. It was during the war also that he discovered that he could paint. He went from demob to the Slade.

The only photograph I ever saw of him was taken at about this time. In it he is standing by the wide doorway of a building, a museum or gallery perhaps. He wears a jersey with his shirt collar out over it, a jacket which must have been tweed, and a scarf. His features then were almost delicate, fine in his long thin face; he looks towards the photographer with tolerant contempt. From his mouth it is not clear whether he was about to be cruel or humorous. Even though the photograph is black and white, you would know that his eyes were blue.

Something about him in the photograph is very English. My mother remarked that his family were never proper Welsh, that it was all just affectation, with the name and everything. We never shared his name. In the time that she and my father were together he did not establish that the Brooklands wife, encouraged by her parents, had been granted a divorce in his absence.

'He couldn't be bothered,' my mother told me. 'Of course, it would have been different if we'd had a son. If one of you had been a boy he would have tried a lot harder.'

In a mews behind Belgrave Square there was a pub called the Star Tavern. In the post-war years it was a place of great celebrity. Milling and thronging in its bars were film stars and embassy people, lawyers and artists, writers and racehorse trainers and Sunday paper gossip columnists; all of them held in the thrall of the hollering Irish charisma, with its charm, oaths, insults and divinity, of the landlord, Paddy Kennedy.

My mother worked in a government office in Belgrave Square. She and her colleagues called in at the Star, as a scene of entertainment, before their tube or buses. One evening she took a drunken Jack back to her room for scrambled eggs. It became habitual. When my sister was born in 1950 my mother pretended to be married with a brass curtain ring. People in the office sent her to Coventry, she said.

At the Slade they thought Jack very good. For the first time in his life he showed application, and they had asked him to stay on and teach a class. He and my mother lived in furnished rooms in Clapham on very little money; in the evenings she had no wish to drink cider and talk of Samuel Palmer. Jack began to stay away from home increasingly; my sister always maintained that she remembered nothing of his presence. He secured commissions to travel and illustrate for Shell guides. My mother took to writing to a man she had met during the war, an agronomist working for the Australian government. It seemed that back in 1946 he had made her an unconditional offer of marriage but, at that date, she had been unwilling to commit to emigration.

There must, however, have been some brief and intermittent rapprochements with Jack. I was born in June of 1955. My mother told me that she spent Christmas Day of 1954 in a hot bath drinking gin. When she found that she could not shift me she went to stay with her mother in Whitstable. I was born in a dim bedroom with lithographs of Canterbury's Westgate and

Bell Harry Tower upon the walls.

My father must have seen me once when I was a newborn infant, before I had a name. They summoned him to the little bungalow and he arrived, drunk, in the taxi hired out by Mr Dunk's garage. He was told that my mother was going to Australia and to let that be an end of it.

The agronomist in Australia developed acute myeloid leukaemia. A sister of his cabled from Canberra to tell my mother when he was gone. My mother took us back to Clapham. It happened that she was a favourite of the landlord, a little wizened man with cycle clips and a belted gabardine. All day long he cycled the quiet South London streets between the Commons, inspecting his many properties and collecting his rents. He found us a proper maisonette; many others were less fortunate in the post war dearth of housing stock.

My mother began looking for employment, remarking that it was a shame that my sister and I were the wrong generation for her to have been widowed in the war. A lot of women got away with that one, she said. She found a job in a post office in a parade of shops not far from Clapham Common. She was good at figures, she enjoyed balancing columns in red and black and all the attendant paraphernalia; the bobbled rubber thimbles for counting notes, snapping bulldog clips and date stamps to bang down hard on order books. It must have been comfortably predictable and methodical for her, after Jack as he was in those days.

In the long school holidays my sister and I were sent to stay with our grandmother. My sister made friends there with facility; she was always out and about, one year even spending a great deal of time with the road gang who were laying tarmac on the lane to Silk's shop. My sister's name was Belinda but my mother said that it had been his choice and shortened it so that she was always Linny or Lin. My grandmother disliked me and favoured Lin, dressing her hair with huge white ribbon bows and telling her that she was dainty and helping her to make cross-stitched tray cloths from a material called binka. Me she criticised for being plump and clumsy. When I tried to make amends by refusing cake from the stand on the tea table she would snap, 'I can't think why you're so fat, you never eat anything.'

When my grandmother recognised that I was able at English she softened towards me to the extent that we read poetry together; she would pause at the end of a verse to draw on a cigarette left resting in the ashtray of Benares brass. Her choice of poems was invariably melancholy, Ralph Hodgson's 'The Bull', 'The Forsaken Merman', another one addressed to a bulldog whose master would never come home from the Great War.

My grandmother had always been a statuesque woman, standing on her dignity in the square-neck costumes with dress clips that she had worn since the forties. But in the summer that I was eleven I saw that she had lost weight rapidly. It became apparent to me that she was bleeding from inside; I wished not to have realised this symptom. Her remarks were more spiteful and unkind, even to Lin, although my sister appeared either not to notice or to care. For her there were men and boys everywhere. Lin exuded sexuality; she had been what my mother called 'bosomy' for years, now she seemed swollen by sex, not just in her breasts but in her hips and her parted lips which she made rough by chewing them. There was a sex smell that came from her too, not least from the top of her head. The odour from her pillows filled the air of our bedroom. The only concern that seemed to trouble Lin was the greasy condition of her hair; several times a day she puffed it despairingly with a little bottle of dry shampoo. In a magazine she had read that washing only made it worse.

My grandmother died in the Cottage Hospital at Whitstable in a ward where an old woman with beribboned pigtails screamed and capered up and down. My mother said that I was old enough to look after myself in the summer holidays anyway. Most days I sat reading with mugs of cocoa into which I dipped Marie biscuits. I got through the books on the living-room shelf, which were Howard Spring novels and Somerset Maugham short stories; then I began going to the library on Lavender Hill where they let me borrow from the adult section.

I had a place at the grammar school. My mother took me to Kinch and Lack, the school outfitters in Artillery Row. My waist was too big for the standard uniform; they said that they would have to order the gymslip specially. On the train back from Victoria to Clapham Junction my mother fretted over the expense.

'If your bloody father had ever given us any money...'

I watched the backs of people's houses passing the train windows; strips of garden, corrugated sheds, bands of bright curtaining, a tortoiseshell cat waiting to be let in. When I was seven she had told me that he was dead. We had made a cake with water icing and silver dragees for a doll's tea party but she had tired of the game and become angry, picking up the miniature cups and saucers and throwing them across the room so that the weak cold tea splashed up the skirting board. 'One day I'll be dead too, like your father, then you'll be sorry.'

'Is he dead?' I asked her, there in the compartment of the train.

'I don't know, but he might as well be. I'd never go to him for anything, the bastard.'

At Clapham County Grammar School they gave you a rough work exercise book with a soft green cover. In the back of it I began to compile a list of everything I knew about my father. I was obsessively neat with my secret list; it was for me a sort of collector's album. I tried Lin but she had nothing to add.

'Don't you ever wonder about him?'

'No, why should I, he's nothing to me.'

'But do you think he might be still alive? Do you think he lives somewhere in London?'

'Not if he still drinks like she says he used to and anyway, I don't give a monkey's either way.'

I gave up with Lin but, by careful timing, I found that I could goad my mother into bitter or impatient reminiscence in which I was able to discover new incidents of his biography.

'He was nothing but a spoilt mother's boy, overindulged from the start. He told me how he broke his leg when he was about three years old. They had to put him in traction and to stop him getting bored and fretful they got the colliery band to come and play on the lawn underneath his bedroom window. He always did think the world owed him a living...'

There was the one photograph of him, kept in the middle drawer of the heavy dark sideboard. When I was alone I used to take it out and hold it in front of me, staring so hard that I could vivify the image and believe that he lived and breathed for me. I felt that he understood me. I do not recall that there was ever a time when I looked upon my father's face with anything but adoration.

'He was never faithful, not from day one, I know that for a fact. He used to be at it with some damned woman from that pub in Pont Street, she carried her own silver swizzle stick round with her, if you please. I knew quite well he used to come straight from her to me, I could smell her on him. He had that way with him, that little boy lost act he used to put on, especially when he was pie-eyed, women used to fall over themselves for him.

He just lapped it up, of course; he took it for granted, because his mother had spoilt him rotten. In the end he stopped bothering even to pretend about what he'd been up to. That's when you really want to worry with a man, if he doesn't even try to pretend any more.'

My mother was ironing while she relayed to me my father's unfaithfulness; she moved the iron with angry jerking movements so that the casing of the flex rubbed against the edge of the board; it was already unravelling to show the wires beneath. She finished the garment and banged the iron upon its stand.

'Husband and father – him, don't make me laugh.'

At school, in the lessons for which I had no facility and did not enjoy – singing and physics and maths and geography – I used to stare out the tall white windows to Wandsworth Common and pass the period by musing over the physical characteristics of my father, none of which had been copied into Lin or me. We were both dark-haired and dark-eyed; our mother's hair was black and her eyes were green, a feature she had told us that men always seemed to go for. Lin was taller than me and slim in the places where she was not swollen with sexuality. As well as having less height I was still constantly plump, so that games and PE lessons, and sometimes even just having to walk along the roads to and from the school, were experiences of misery.

Sometimes by lucky chance a random event would trigger my mother to recall some new aspect of her life with my father. One evening the London news carried a story about maternity services; she was impatient with the plight of those adversely affected in the report.

'And they think they're badly off,' she said to the sincere faces talking and nodding on the television screen. 'When I went into labour with Lin, all the bloody hospitals were full. He was nowhere to be found, of course. Sholie, the woman from upstairs, she had to come with me in the ambulance. They drove me all round London until they got me a bed at the Princess Beatrice, and that was as posh as you like. He didn't turn up for two days and when he did he was blind drunk. I looked up and saw him weaving down the middle of the ward and I thought, oh, my God, it's not fair, it's just not bloody fair. All these blasted well-to-do women with their perfectly pressed nightdresses and every one of them had these beautiful crisp pyjamas to wear for doing the exercise classes. I had nothing, nothing but a hospital gown. I told him to bring me in some underwear so he went to Harrods and bought me a pair of silk drawers, one bloody pair.'

'What was wrong with them?'

'What was wrong with them – one pair of knickers, when you've just had a baby, you work it out. God, he was a useless bastard.'

'What colour were they?'

'What colour were what?'

'The silk knickers, what colour were they?'

'I don't bloody know, do I, after all these years.'

My mother had kept none of Jack's possessions except for two books. One of these, an early sketchbook from the Slade, was subsequently thrown away. She had let us use the spare pages for painting when we were small and later she disposed of the damp, stuck block we had made of it. The second of the books was *Dream Days*, a collection of stories by Kenneth Grahame. The cover was blue, stamped with a twining art nouveau design of briar and blossom; in the centre there was the suggestion of the arch of a doorway framing the initials of the publishers – TNS, Thomas Nelson & Sons. The design was repeated on the end papers within. My father had written his name – John (Jack) ap Rhys Owen – on the page facing the frontisplate. In the picture plate beautiful, ephemeral children in sailor suits gazed through a grove of trees towards a sacred hilltop castle, rising up out of a mist. Their hair and hat ribbons were lifted by a breeze; you knew that this breeze would be soft and fragrant and without menace.

When I first found *Dream Days* and its inscription I asked my mother whose it was.

'Whose d'you think? It was your father's. I don't know why I don't chuck it out. Tatty old thing.'

In the first year at Clapham County there was a lesson they called Language; it was taken prior to learning Latin. We were taught about the origins of the English language, about place names and how the names of trades had given people their surnames. After one lesson I went to ask the teacher at her desk and she explained to me that ap Rhys was son of Rhys, that in modern days it was less usual and was often foreshortened into Pryce.

'Why do you ask? Your name isn't Welsh.' She piled her papers together and snapped her handbag closed as the end of lesson bell drilled.

'I just wondered.'

It was over the counter of the post office that my mother met her permanent man friend. His name was Ron; he was a driving instructor for the British School of Motoring. He used the post office branch to pay in his takings, ten-shilling and pound notes and silver coin in a canvas bag. At home my mother announced that she was signing up for driving lessons. Ron had a wife and children in Tooting and so their first meetings were illicit and at odd hours.

Watching Ron sitting on the sofa in our flat, I thought that he slightly resembled a frog, because of the way his eyes bulged and the position in which he sat with his short legs bent in their narrow trousers. He had brown curly hair which had begun to recede; he was some years younger than my mother. She had taken to wearing lipstick again, a crimson shade named on the base 'Gay Geranium'. I wished, for her own sake, that she would shave her legs above the knees. Ron dressed in casual shirts and because his stomach was large he belted his trousers low down. One of his two characteristic habits was to make an extended grinding noise with his teeth to emphasise statements or to express surprise. His teeth were notably fine and white despite his heavy smoking. The other habit was the repetition of rhymes and phrases which served him as recurring punch lines in conversation; there was 'Owing to the wind and rain, Christmas will be late again' and 'All coppers are bar stewards'.

During the first weeks of Ron's visits to our flat I felt some sympathy towards him, I saw him as a pathetic and vaguely embarrassing little man. When the extent of my mother's partiality for him became obvious I saw that there was no longer any need to feel sorry for Ron.

When we heard the door bell late at night I said to Lin, 'Is that him, again?'

She snapped back at me, 'Why shouldn't she have someone? It's none of your business.'

Lin was animated in Ron's company; they exchanged ripostes and repeated jokes of marked unkindness from a television show named *The Comedians* which they both enjoyed. Once when Lin and I were standing beside each other Ron called to my mother, 'Look at these two standing side by side, it's like Laurel and bleeding Hardy.'

When Lin was at home she was sometimes allowed to join my

mother and Ron to drink the bottles of Young's beer which he brought clinking in on his late-night visits. They threw cigarettes to each other across the room, rather than getting up to offer the packet. My mother chain-smoked on these occasions. Ron would say 'Blimey, Mo, what d'you do with them, eat them?'

As the evening wore on and the rapport between Lin and Ron increased, my mother's mood would become edgy and irritable; she would make an exaggerated show of emptying ashtrays and clearing away their glasses. Then Lin, calculating that she had pushed my mother far enough, would give a small pleased smile and leave them alone together on the brown sofa.

Sometimes on Saturday afternoons when I was doing homework at the table Ron would walk through to the kitchen, eyeing me warily, although I consciously tried never to look disapproving or embarrassed. 'Thought your mum deserved a cup of tea,' he would say and return with a tin tray of cups and a packet of Embassy cigarettes.

In certain subjects at school I was an outstanding pupil. At first the teachers had treated me with wary reserve because Lin had been unruly, rude and a troublemaker. She left during the year that I began; she went to Pitman's College for a shorthand and typing course and then on to a rapid succession of jobs where, invariably, she became involved with at least one man. Most recently she had joined an academic support department at the London School of Economics. For a few weeks a young fair man used to call for her; he was a student activist named Ted. Ted and I ate McVities ginger cake together.

'When is Ted coming again?' I asked her one day.

'He's not, I've packed him up. I got sick of it; he was always going on about the bleeding Greek colonels.'

I worked very hard at all my subjects at school because it brought me praise and because there was nothing else in my life that I liked very much. I also applied myself with extra dedication when I began to suffer from recurrent bouts of tonsillitis, which frightened me and filled me with dread. Every time I used to think that I was going to die. When the pain in my throat was at its most intense I used to wonder how much pain human bodies could tolerate and whether and when they just gave up and died. I had heard that animals crawled away to die. I would listen for my heartbeat in my head against the pillow, fearing that at some point it would not repeat. I used to imagine essays that I had handed in being marked, but me being already dead.

I did not discuss these fears with anyone. I had tried, with Lin, but she was derisive. 'You're round the twist,' she said. I knew that my mother would be impatient and dismissive; worse, that by attempting to impress upon her how real my anxieties were, I would only make myself feel those anxieties the more, while she herself remained unmoved. I was, in any case, a secretive child by nature. It was silence and the crafts of concealment that won me Jack.

So, by immersing myself in the school subjects I would pretend, for as long as possible, that an illness was not going to happen again. I always knew, with a dreadful inevitability, when the infection was coming on. I would try to resist it with extra study and with diversions and home-made cures of chocolate bars or bits of ice picked from the freezer compartment; I took long walks across Wandsworth Common or chose new books from the third-form paperback library which was operated from a large brown cupboard. Some hot nights I would read through, finishing a book at dawn; but the course of the illness always had its way, as I had known it must.

My mother viewed the illnesses as personal inconvenience. 'You can't expect me to take time off work,' she would say. 'Get yourself to the doctor's again.'

The elderly doctor's surgery was the ground floor of his house on the West Side of Clapham Common. He depressed my tongue with instruments kept in a beaker of diluted Dettol disinfectant. The taste to me was not unpleasant, my mouth and throat being so hot and full of infection.

'I'll give you another scrip for penicillin. Make sure you take it all, and try to drink or gargle, there's a lot of debris there.' He accented the word in the French way; on his desk there was a perpetual calendar of brass which extended to a new millennium. The doctor was stern, he reminded me of some minor character from a wartime film. I did not dare to ask him about dying but I was comforted to sense that he was kind towards me.

When the tonsils are severely inflamed, it is impossible to swallow anything, even saliva is too painful. Because, so often, I could not eat, I began to grow thinner. I missed almost a whole school year. When, after a long bout of illness, I returned to repeat the fourth form, the games mistress said she hoped she could expect to see me run much faster on the netball court from now on.

We were streamed into sets for different lessons. My Latin teacher said that she had never had a student like me; in English one of my essays was taken away for a competition. I made friends with a bony blonde girl named Alison. Alison was never still, she was constantly restless and animated by a nervy energy. She was so thin that her legs were merely the shape of her bones and yet she took six spoons of sugar in her tea and brought brown paper bags of doorstep sandwiches to eat on her two bus journeys to school.

One morning break when we were sitting on the lost property box reading an Avon catalogue the Latin teacher sought me out, 'Literae Humaniores,' she said.

Alison and I regarded her blankly.

'We have just had confirmation, we put your name forward for the scholarship exam and sent in some of your work. Oxford have agreed to let you sit the paper, even though it will be two years early.'

I was not sure what she was talking about but because her habitual earnestness was lit by pleasure I said thank you.

'We'll write home,' she said. 'I'll organise it straight away, with the school secretary.'

'That must be good then,' said Alison.

I said that I supposed so and we resumed our perusal of the catalogue pages.

Alison lived on a council estate behind the Battersea Dogs' Home at Nine Elms. She was savvy and quick-witted; when she was ten her mother had unexpectedly produced two more children in rapid succession and Alison became self-reliant, playing out on the balconies and walkways and concrete aprons of the estate and in the surrounding streets where there was already demolition for the coming of the New Covent Garden.

I had never played in the street before, and we had great fun together. Looking back, it was an odd mixture of the childish and the prepubescent. With enthusiasm we joined in the nuisance games like Knocking down Ginger that the estate children played. We sat swinging our legs on low walls by chalked pavements, eating the sweets from Jamboree bags and brightly coloured penny chews. At the same time we were often deep in contemplation of the states of love and sexual attraction that we heard enunciated in soul music, or scathing in our disparagement of the lives and tasks of the women in the flats that surrounded us. It seemed that women, once they were settled in a marriage, existed in a world where things spilled out and spilled over. Their hard-skinned soles overlapped the edge of their mule sandals, hair escaped from under scarves, slack stomachs and

breasts overflowed garments, groceries spilled from carrier bags,
children fought to wriggle free from a pram harness or a hand's
grasp, always there were messes spilled and dirt trodden that
must be mopped and wiped. Women leant on their balconies
and watched other people moving, without aspiration. They
were slack, perhaps because their lives had lost the tight excitement and expectant promise they once and briefly had.

For all her daylight freedom, Alison's parents were particularly strict about her fulfilling the household chores that she was
set, and about her coming-home time in the evening; at eight
o'clock she must enter the lift for the seventh floor of the tower
block and the darkening balcony from which you could glimpse
the river and the illumined sign of Dolphin Square. Her father
would stand waiting on the seventh landing for the lift to ascend.
My mother imposed no such restrictions on me; if it was not a
night when Ron was expected she would go to bed early with
a red rubber hot water bottle and a book of crossword puzzles.
When Alison invited me to stay on Friday nights my mother
made no demur; not so long afterwards I was able to exploit her
disinterested attitude in full measure.

On Saturday mornings Alison was tasked with taking the
family's laundry to the Nine Elms wash baths, transporting the
capacious plastic launderette bags in her brother's pram. Sometimes the lifts were out of order and between us we would bump
the pram down the many flights of new brutalism concrete. On
the landings the corners smelled of urine and were strewn with
the charred match boxes left by children making flaming missiles.

The architecture of the Nine Elms wash baths burgeoned
with the improving impetus of Victorian civic philanthropy. The
terracotta brickwork was embellished with garlands and urns
and classical masks. Inside there were majolica wall tiles and

mosaic floors, polished brass fittings and teak benches. Alison said that in one section you bought a bathe with a towel and soap hired, but only old men and funny men went there now, she thought. 'My mum always says to keep well out of it.'

The laundry section of the wash baths was the preserve of female company. The superintendent was a small bird-eyed woman; her hair was dyed ink-black and worn in a 1940s-style snood at the base of her neck.

'Morning, girls, come to do Mum's wash, have we?'

Two other women sat on the wooden benches. In the disposition of their wearied limbs and the large ungainly bulk of their mainly fawn clothing and their dull eyes they resembled old soldiers, resting after a campaign. One of them had leg bandages which could have been puttees.

'That's right.' Alison was intent upon inspecting the change her mother had given her, calculating whether by doubling up the load at the drier stage she could save enough money to buy herself a packet of ten cigarettes on the way home. Alison favoured the menthol kind but if she could not afford a whole packet we visited the newsagent who sold threepenny singles and assured us, each time, that it was better to be born lucky than born rich.

I helped her to load the wash into one of the big blue machines that had been screwed to the mosaic floor.

'How's your boy then, Doreen?' one of the old soldier women asked the superintendent.

'My son? Don't ask. I was in the Cricketers last night and she came in, with her husband. No shame.'

She looked to Alison: 'You know my boy Danny, don't you?'

'Not me, no.' Alison turned away, drumming her bony fingers on the metal lid of the machine. I knew that she did know Danny, we both did; we talked to him sometimes while he was out mending his motor scooter.

'He's with the Electric Board, doing his City and Guilds, you must have seen him around. Now he's got himself hitched up with an older woman.' The superintendent turned towards me and I felt surprise that she deemed me old or informed enough to be included in the conversation. 'Dreadful it is, shocking.'

After each sentence she patted the crimson mouth corners of her lipstick with a fingertip; the nylon fabric of her overall whispered as she moved her arms.

'And married too, is she, Doreen?' the other bench woman put in, the glint in her eyes showing that she was keen to stir up the indignation further.

'Too right she is, I just told you, he was there last night, the husband. She can't get enough, the bitch. She's a ruddy nympho. Pardon me, girls.'

'I don't suppose you're telling these anything they don't already know, not nowadays.'

Alison was watching for the powder light on the machine to come on. Under her breath she said, 'Let's hope to God we never turn into one of them when we're old. You'd shoot yourself first, wouldn't you?'

'That's true, they know it all these days, don't you, girls. Have your cake and eat it. And you don't ever have to get caught either, not now, when you can take a pill to stop it.'

'That's right. Buy me and stop one,' said Alison.

'Hark at you. Come here and take the end of this sheet for me.'

Alison and the superintendent stood pulling and folding sheets, walking towards each other with the ends when the requisite size was reached. I had tried it one week but had lost hold when Doreen had stretched and twitched the cloth and so I was not asked again. Alison was expert, knowing instinctively the choreography of the task and holding fast to the corners when they were tugged.

'So, girls, you got boyfriends?'

I shook my head. Alison said, 'Might have.'

'I thought you would. It's because you're a blonde, men can never resist a blonde. What's he like?'

'All right, I suppose.'

'I hope you don't let him.'

One of the bench women raised her head as if from a reverie. 'They'll never respect you if you do.'

The superintendent turned to me. 'Ah, look at her there, all wide-eyed. You're too quiet and shy for all this, aren't you, love?'

'She's all right,' Alison said.

'Here it comes.' The bench women were nodding at a younger woman who was entering, pulling her wash behind her in a basket on wheels. Her heels tapped on the mosaic and her newly dressed hair was swept back and lacquered into curls. She eyed the seated women critically for a moment and then said to one, 'Blimey, close your legs, girl, your meat's smelling.'

The other woman guffawed and the superintendent clicked her tongue in disapproval.

Alison said, 'They're such dirty old bags in here, they make me sick. Come on, let's go and tap the phone instead while the wash is doing.'

By these words Alison did not mean to suggest that we listened in to the conversations of others – although we always welcomed a crossed line – rather, it was a method she had acquired of literally tapping up and down the cradle of old black composition telephones in a sequence corresponding to a number. In most cases it would effect a connection. Alison would scan the directories in the hope of finding a famous name. She had also

22

perfected a method to reach the GPO recruitment line with its own recorded song which began 'Hey, hey, hey telephone girl'. She would sing back to the jingle, gyrating and dancing in the small space of the telephone box.

'Go on, find us a number from the books.' While she began to clack at the receiver rest I opened a directory. 'See if you can find us a teacher's number, we'll give them a heavy breather. Try the Latin teacher's, go on, in the A–D.'

I ran my finger down the columns for the Latin teacher and, in so doing, I found the listing for my father's name. Crowded into the telephone box on the bright Battersea pavement, where the ornate bricks of the baths threw back the warmth of the sun, I smiled in recognition at the entry on the printed page. I wondered why I had not thought to look before. His address was 33 Oakley Street, SW3.

'Well, get a move on, have you found it?'

'Not her. She's not in here. I'll try someone else.'

In the afternoon we went to Clapham Junction and roamed the departments of Arding and Hobbs until the millinery assistants told us to leave. Coming out of the side door onto Lavender Hill we saw that a crowd had gathered outside the record store named the Slipped Disc.

'Let's have a butcher's,' Alison said, propelling us through the traffic.

The singer Desmond Dekker was signing copies of his newly released record. We had no money to buy one but a member of the entourage handed us each a copy. Looking at me, he said, 'Free – if you give me your phone number.' I thought he must be speaking to someone else. I looked about me.

'He meant you, thickhead,' said Alison as we walked away, 'God, you're so slow sometimes. You were well in there. He really fancied you.'

I was dumbfounded. I saw the world from within the outline that people like my grandmother and the games mistresses had drawn around me. They had told me that I was fat and ungainly and unlovely, and therefore, I assumed, I was unlovable. It had not occurred to me that I might ever be found attractive. When I looked in a mirror I always stood to one side so that only half of me was reflected.

'Strewth, wake up, girl, do,' said Alison and I felt a lip edge of confident pleasure begin to curl. She was speaking through chunks of nougat, biting off a solid bar. 'And talking of doing it and all, I might as well tell you, I've got a boyfriend now, Beccles. And I'm not really a virgin any more.'

Stewart Beccles was the tall, serious Jamaican boy from her estate. I was astonished by the nonchalance with which she imparted this admission. Further, I saw that I would have expected my friend to have been somehow changed by such an event, yet she was not.

'Where did you do it, and when, when did you do it?'

'On the stairs. Last Tuesday. It's all right as it goes, you should try it.'

Without delay I began to test the theory that Alison, and by inference, the man from the record company had advanced, gauging in the eyes of men that passed me in the street and in cars their response to the way that I looked. When I saw how they reacted to me it was headier than any alcohol. I stopped covering myself up with layers of cardigans and coats.

Two days later the council announced that due to the coming of the New Covent Garden market, Alison's family were to be rehoused to an estate on the site of the old Croydon Airfield. Her mother was delighted, she said that it would be healthier, with green spaces and a residents' club. I cried over Alison leaving and she cried over Beccles.

*

My consolation lay in the list at the back of the exercise book. I had written down my father's address. Now that I could be sure that men liked looking at me I wanted him to see me as well.

Ron was surprised when I offered to brush out his car. 'What's this, Bob a Job Week?'

As I walked down the hall with the brush and pan I heard him say to my mother: 'She's really bucked up since she lost all that weight. She'll give her sister a run for her money, looks-wise.'

I had offered to sweep out the car because I knew that Ron kept an A–Z in the door compartment. Although I was charged with excitement I set myself first to sweep steadily at the carpet where he flicked his cigarette ash, just in case the two of them were watching me. When it was done I opened out the A–Z on the floor of the car; I found the index and then the page and the location in relation to Albert Bridge. With a surge of happiness for the neatly labelled roads I saw how straightforward it would all be.

A letter arrived to say that my essay had won the competition.

'What d'you win?' asked Lin.

'Book tokens.'

'Great,' she said, with sarcasm.

Lin and my mother were each and both preoccupied. Problems had arisen with Ron's wife; she had told him that she needed more money. My mother said that he would have to moonlight at night for a security firm. 'He's deadbeat tired as it is,' she fretted.

Lin's period was late. She was booked for a clinic in the

women's hospital at Clapham South. There was a hard frost and patches of ice remained on the paths of Clapham Common. Lin slipped and broke the urine specimen bottle she had in the pocket of her sheepskin coat. She turned back home and missed the appointment. When she came in her tights were torn and dirty and her eyes like those of a small animal that lives in woodland. I wanted to demonstrate sympathy towards her but I knew that she would repel me. I asked her if she would like a cup of coffee but she said that she would rather have a fucking drink and went to lie down. I returned to my homework, which was 'The Pardoner's Tale'.

In the evening my mother asked me, 'You wouldn't mind, would you, if Ron moved in with us for a bit?'

I thought how horrible it would be. Him smoking when he went to the lavatory so that there was the smell there afterwards and often a cigarette end floating in the water of the bowl. The noises from him and my mother, grunting in her bedroom. His grey nylon socks with maroon patterns visible beneath the short trouser legs, and the two undisciplined Alsatian-cross dogs which he sometimes brought with him.

'No, of course not,' I said.

That night I took *Dream Days* from the shelf and put it under my pillow; next day I took it to school and kept it hidden in my desk. For a time I waited for my mother to notice that it was missing but I do not believe that she ever did.

On the first night of Ron living with us my mother served us fish fingers with instant mashed potato and tinned spaghetti. She must have felt the need to excuse herself for she announced, defensively, 'I can't be expected to muck about in the kitchen, not when I've been working all day.'

'You going to wash up for your mum, then?' Ron asked me as he lit a cigarette and blew a fan of smoke across his smeared plate.

'No,' my mother put in hastily, 'no, she and I will do it together. We need to have a little talk.'

I thought it might be about the Literae Humaniores scholarship. The school had sent home a letter explaining the arrangements for the exam.

The tray-shaped draining board, bolted to the side of the sink, was very small, you had to dry things promptly to give the washer-up the space to put the next item down. As I snatched up a plate she asked, 'Have you thought about getting a little job, on Saturdays maybe? Somewhere down Northcote Road or the Junction. It would be nice to have a bit more pocket money now, wouldn't it? Now that you're taking a pride in yourself.'

I was embarrassed on her behalf. Not just for her underlying motivation in wanting me out of the flat more often but because of the sham, flimsy ploy from which she had fashioned her excuse. I wished that she could have done better. The cutlery made the unpleasant, scraping sound that it always makes when picked up from a metal surface in a bunch.

'All right, I'll see what I can find. Have you read the letter from school yet, they were asking me today?'

'Give me a chance, do. They're always sending some damn thing home from that place.'

I took my homework to my bedroom, it was sines and cosines and quite beyond my understanding. I began shading in the little boxes of the tables with a soft pencil, enumerating the shops along the Northcote Road to which I might apply.

In growing up, and sometimes in after life, if it is lived under personal or other restrictions, there is a bracing sense of liberation that comes with the notion of disobedience or of consciously flouting the rules or the recommendations of another person. It is fearful yet exciting, foregoing timidity allows more admiration of oneself and the self as seen by others. Sometimes, on the edge of sleep, dreams came in which I fell, sometimes just over a kerb, sometimes from the great height of a bridge; physicians say that it resembles, fractionally, episodes of *petit mal*. Always the sensation of falling made me jerk awake, afraid and dry-mouthed. Sometimes I wondered how it would be if I let the fall continue, what would I have seen. In the matter of a job, bored and idly doodling on the pages of *School Mathematics*, the pleasurable realisation came to me that I could consciously discount my mother's wheedling suggestions of Northcote Road or Clapham Junction. I could go straight across the river to SW3.

Several times a week the Latin teacher would seek me out saying, 'Let's find ourselves a quiet corner,' and, her patient manner moderating her suppressed excitement for my opportunity, she prepared me for the scholarship paper. It had been decided that I must continue with the O-level subjects as normal and so she borrowed timetable gaps within the ordinary school day; she brought us fruit gums in a box to eat.

Because my mother had not read the letter, placing it instead in the seashell-decorated wooden rack on the mantelpiece, I almost missed the scholarship exam. At a morning assembly on that day, I was sitting as usual upon the hard bench, minutely inspecting my nails as teenage girls are wont to do. Our form's places were beside the honours board, remembering in gilt lettering girls of the twenties and thirties whose Christian names, Violets and Ethels and Mauds, made them seem irretrievably historic. I sensed some commotion at the end of the row and then, with all heads turned to stare, I was ushered out of the hall.

'What on earth are you doing here?' my form teacher asked. 'You are supposed to be in the exam at half past ten.'

In the corridor, the Latin teacher, whose face was white and drawn, the form teacher and the school secretary surrounded me in agitation: '...Such a privilege...' said one, '...there's only three children in the whole country sitting this paper today.'

Between them they decided that they must not interrupt the headmistress in assembly; a taxi was called and the mufflered driver took me to an institutional building somewhere off Gower Street. He asked if I was being punished for something.

An elderly man in a tweed jacket was to adjudicate. He looked at me as if he expected me to do something vulgar; I sensed it was because I was wearing eye make-up. The other candidates were a girl whose father was at the Ghanaian embassy and a boy whose clothes and manner seemed so outdated that first of all I felt protective towards him. However, when he spoke to me and to the other girl, who was so nervous that she seemed about to be ill, he was most assured and patronising. The adjudicator, whose teeth were stained, showed him favour. I did not find the questions to be especially difficult; my teacher had anticipated the content from Books I to VI of *The Aeneid* and had further rehearsed me in *Metamorphoses*, Books I to IX. When I put up my hand to request more paper the elderly man was terse. At home I did not tell them that I had taken the exam.

On the Saturday morning when I went to seek work I borrowed the make-up from Lin's dressing table while she was still asleep. Her mascara was of the block kind, she spat in it to mix it. Sometimes, in consequence, it grew a layer of mould on top which I would clean away, mixing the block freshly with tap water. I considered thus that I was doing her a service by borrowing it.

Lin stirred, bleary. Her latest boyfriend managed a pub belonging to his uncle; a modern premises near Wandsworth Bridge, it had a concrete terrace with tables set beside the river.

Lin had stayed late, helping to clear up.

'Get us a coffee, a frothy one with boiling milk; make sure you really boil it. And chocolate biscuits, if she's bought any more.'

She sat up for the coffee and eyed me suspiciously. 'Where are you going?'

'Just shopping. I thought I might go down Kings Road.'

'Get you,' and then, 'got any money?'

'No, not really. I can just look, I suppose.'

She regarded me pityingly but then, grumbling as she stretched for her handbag, she gave me two pound notes.

'Piss off then,' she said, 'I'm going back to sleep.'

Halfway along the Kings Road I found the Great Gear Trading Company. Once a vast garage premises, it had been converted into an indoor market housing stalls which sold clothing and jewellery and the little bottles of scented oils in which patchouli vanquished all other smells. When I asked about a job a stall-holder told me to go and find the manager in the office. The office was very narrow and painted orange.

A man was sitting on the edge of the desk staring abstract-edly into the small space. 'I'm Jimmy McGibbon,' he replied to my enquiry. 'Strictly speaking I am an actor, but in between times, yes, I do manage this zoo.'

Jimmy stood up and prowled up and down the narrow space as he talked, hands behind his back. He was very slim, with short hair that curled in a fringe like a Roman's in an epic film; his eyes were pale grey-blue. He moved like a dancer or a boxer. He wore a waisted canvas jacket and a black T-shirt and jeans which were very tight but bulged at the groin.

'We could do with someone in here. A floater if you like. The stallholders are always disappearing somewhere, leaving things open and unattended. Hang on, music for the masses.'

On a shelf there was a stereo system; he took out a Leonard

Cohen LP and set it upon the turntable. Although we could watch the revolutions, we heard no music in the office; distantly it began through the speakers outside in the market space.

'You're very beautiful. Do you ever think of having any contacts done?'

'What are they?'

'You know, publicity photos, talent stuff, modelling and so on?'

'No.'

'Don't look so worried. I'm not trying to get it on with you or anything. I've had my orgasm today already, thanks. It's just my agent's always asking me to be on the look-out for any fresh-faced talent on the Kings Road. So, you're still a schoolgirl then, are you? I bet you get a lot of tedious gits asking you about your gymslip. Do you still get taught Shakespeare at school nowadays?'

'Yes.'

'Good thing, I suppose.' He was abstracted again, watching the record turn with music that we could only faintly hear.

I waited for a time and then asked, 'May I have the job?'

'Course you can, if you want it. Start next week.'

Out in Kings Road I turned left, in the direction of Oakley Street. I wondered what my father did on Saturdays. All around me were men of more or less the right age, many as a part of couples; he could be one among them. Walking in front of me there was a man and a woman with a girl child and a boy child. They were perhaps ten and twelve years old, the boy was quite staid but the girl, hanging on to her father's hand, danced and jigged about like a puppet. They paused, waiting to cross Shaw-field Street, and I stopped behind them. The girl turned and looked at me and I saw, in her smooth round face, how desolate I would be if I found that my father had other children. She had a freckled nose and for a second I wanted to hit her. In order not to follow the family any further I turned and crossed over Kings Road. In doing so I saw that a hamburger restaurant named the American Dream had a postcard in the window advertising for part-time waitresses. I assessed the dual advantages of having a job here as well as at the market; I could spend more time in Chelsea close to and looking for my father and less time at home, with Ron now in residence.

The restaurant smelt of coffee and onions and cigarette smoke. A few tables were occupied. In the window sat the two manageresses: Julie, who was heavily built with backcombed hair and Cleopatra eyeliner, and tall, thin Renata, who was Austrian.

'We'll interview you now,' they said. 'Can you carry three plates at once?'

'I'm not sure, I've never tried, I don't think.'

'It's easy.' Renata fetched three plates and held one in each hand and one resting on her extended arm. 'See? Three is good, four like this is chancing.'

'Okay.' I was surprised to find that I could do it too.

'You've passed,' said Julie. 'The pay's crap but you get to keep all your tips. We give you a T-shirt and you have to wear your own jeans. Make sure they are tight, especially on a Saturday night, and then you'll get all the home-going footie fans tipping better.'

As soon as you turn into Oakley Street you can see, far away at the river end, the pillars of Albert Bridge, promising like a proscenium arch. The street itself, and the pavements, are wide, the houses tall. I established that I was on the odd numbers side. I saw that number 33 had a green door and a series of bell pushes; above it there was a balcony with ironwork. That first time, when I looked at my father's house, I blushed with guilt.

I felt sure that somewhere eyes must be upon me, watching me spy and able to read my most private thoughts, but there was nobody to be seen.

I took the bus across the river almost every day, either to work or simply to walk in the area closest to Oakley Street. When my school day ended I rushed to change my clothes in the noisome lavatory block where once I had been afraid of the bigger, smoking girls who crammed into a cubicle and passed between them a single cigarette. In Kings Road I had bought narrow-legged vintage Levis from the Jean Machine shop and platform boots which added five inches to my height. My hair was very long and straight and shiny. I used a small round pot of gloss from Mary Quant to make my lips shine too, like glacé kid. One afternoon, when I was hurrying through the school gates for Northcote Road and the 49 bus, my English teacher stopped me. She had doggish features and was round-shouldered in her twinset cardigan.

'Where are you off to in such a rush?'

'For the bus, I have to go to work.'

She regarded me with some regret. 'Here is where you should be working, Susanna, this is such an important time for you.'

But I was careless of her concerns; I knew my capabilities, I was able to do much of my homework on the bus. The week before I had translated a passage from Catullus in a traffic jam on Battersea Bridge. I was awarded full marks for it and at the foot of the page the comment: 'A beautifully considered piece of work. Well done!'

I set myself to learn the streets of Chelsea. The area that I selected ran from Beaufort Street to Markham Square. I treated it as if it was the lines and acts of a play. I was very quick on the uptake; soon I had not only the street names by heart but the incidental signifiers of businesses and inhabitants. I learned where certain cars habitually parked, the sun-warmed spots where cats lounged, the range of ornaments on a windowsill, the basement flat where an old man with a shawl around his shoulders had hundreds of model soldiers laid out upon a board. Up and down and through and back I went, working the streets like a tapestry needle. I placed Givan's Irish linen, Swan Court, the antique sellers where there was a waterfall clock marked 'not for sale' as the centrepiece. I found Ossie Clark's in Radnor Walk and the offices of the *Chelsea Post*. In Margaretta Terrace, behind Oakley Street, a fortunate child was put to bed each evening in an attic with rocking horse-patterned curtains. It was, I see, an extension of the notes in the exercise book, a further obsessive compulsion to amass as much detail as I could about anything remotely connected to my father. Very soon I was attached to that collection of Chelsea streets with the sort of fondness which I suppose people must feel towards the university city where they have flourished and achieved.

For the delight and the guilty anticipation of it, I used to leave Oakley Street until last. I knew that sooner or later I would see my father. When I lay down to sleep each night I imagined how it would happen. If I was feeling low I punished myself with visions of him amid a bevy of small blonde girl children, spilling out of the green front door; they were dressed in Fair Isle cardigans and Russell and Bromley shoes and they clamoured and won his attention with the insistent, spoilt piping of their voices. Or I taunted myself with images of him with some tall and luscious, heavy-lidded redhead; she was draping herself across him as they paused beside the iron railings. I saw him murmur to her and kiss her, and put his hand inside her coat. I smelt the strength of her perfume which he would be inhaling. On my best days I saw just him, leaning on the doorstep as he leant in the photograph but looking, not at the camera, but at me.

From the pavement it was not possible to read the names on the bell-push labels. I recognised the two or three cars which parked regularly on that side of the broad street. Soon afterwards I discovered that the residents of the Borough of Kensington and Chelsea were given coloured paper parking discs to display on their windscreens; on these circles of paper there was a dotted line for inserting the name of the entitled householder. It was very simple then. Jack's car was the big old Citroën, two-tone in blue and grey. And, before long, my unshakeable belief that one day he would be there when I passed by was justified.

I had just finished the Sunday afternoon shift at the restaurant, which ran from noon until five o'clock. Nobody else liked it but I volunteered because on Sunday afternoons my mother and Ron either went for what they called a lie down or they watched an old film on the sofa. I knew that they felt compelled to invite me to share in their box of Good News chocolates. I did not want to take one but if I refused my mother was huffy and affronted. I walked down Kings Road, past the town hall and the carpet seller, the chemist with his poster about Venice sinking, the Eight Bells and shuttered Givan's. When I turned into Oakley Street I drew breath sharply and involuntarily I smiled to the darkening Chelsea afternoon. There was the figure of a man beside the Citroën. As I approached him the chink of coins from the day's tips in my pocket seemed very loud and my every step in the platform boots sounded as though around an amphitheatre. My feet appeared to meet the ground sooner, as though the pavement had become angled, slanting upwards to meet me.

From ten houses' distance there was no doubt that it was him: my father from the photograph. He was as tall as I had expected and, opening the tailgate of the old car, he lifted his arm in an arc of easy grace. His hair fell forward on his forehead. I consumed him with my eyes until he might have burned. I contemplated willing him to turn and notice me but I did not yet wish to test that alchemy, I wanted only to be allowed to gaze at him. I thought that he was a beautiful man. I wished that I could stand on the balcony above to watch him as though he and I were the only two in a theatre or a church. My father remained calmly intent upon his task. He leaned into the interior of the car and the bones and the lines of his face were illumined by the pale bulb as if it was candlelight. I could have wept for recognition although I made no outward sign.

Of my two workplaces I liked the Great Gear Trading Company best. One of the traders was a woman named Lalla. Lalla's appearance was striking, with violet blue eyes; in earlier years she had made her living as a film extra at Shepperton Studios. Now she lived in a marriage of some disengagement in a comfortable flat in Prince of Wales Drive beside Battersea Park. There was a son, Julian. Julian attended Westminster School during the week and looked after his mother's clothing stall on Saturdays. Julian and I were the same age but for four months; he became, at once, the friend who replaced Alison. From the other, each of us wished only for friendship and, because there was no competition or sexual tension, we were able to confide and best advise without fear or favour, as though we had been of the same gender.

In his appearance, especially as he walked towards you from a distance, Julian resembled one of those paper dressing dolls where outfits must be cut out and fitted around the cardboard figure by folding over tabs. It was the shape of clothes that young men wore at that time, tight-fitting jumpers or tank tops with big shirt collars out over, above wide, parallel-leg trousers and shoes with rounded toes and a platform sole. Their hairstyles were shaped to the head and neck with fine feathered strands at the crown; these strands trembled like fern leaves with sensitivity to gesture or movement.

Julian's father, Peter, was the managing director of a firm that made cardboard packaging. He took no part in the life of his wife and son that revolved around Kings Road. Sometimes, Julian told me, his father decided that the atmosphere and general lifestyle was unsuitable and unhealthy for his teenage son. 'Nancyish' was a word that he used. He would take Julian off with him to trade conferences in the Midlands or for weekends of golf or walking in Snowdonia. In the summer ahead he had booked the two of them on a water sports holiday. Julian loved his father and wished that things could be otherwise in his parents' marriage but he told me that he found the activities trying.

'It's seriously tough going. It's not the actual stuff that we do, that can be okay, really. It's my dad working so hard at it, he's determined to make life into what he sees as normal and you just know it can never turn out like he wants it to.'

The recurring topic of our conversations was sex; we had a disarmed openness in our discussions. Julian was desperate to have complete intercourse. He said that he had done other stuff which, if you added it up, almost equalled the same, but he wanted the act in its entirety.

'I want to do it properly, you know, take time and everything. Have you done it properly?'

We were sitting in the Picasso café on Kings Road. We had taken to meeting there after school to do homework; a number of our O-level choices were the same.

'I'm not sure, sort of, I think.'

'You must know if you have.'

'Well, I suppose so, but nothing really happened.'

'Didn't you like it?'

'Not much.'

I thought back to the night in question. A boy from the Nine Elms estate had taken me home in a car although he was not old enough to have a licence. We had stopped in Windmill Drive on Clapham Common and he had suggested that we got into the back. Straight away he had given me a lot of instructions in a tone which was petulant and verged upon a whine. I did not like that there was so much of teeth and saliva in his kissing. I preferred dry kisses, of the polite, cheek, visiting-relation kind but delivered on the lips with soft persistence. Looking out through the car window I had been momentarily terrified by the sight of a duck or some other water bird landing clumsily on the dark sheet of the pond. Headlight glare from the avenue caught the pale underside of its wings and made it strange and ghostly. The boy said that he had to make sure and come outside; it sounded as though he were reading instructions from the label of a tin.

'I don't think it counted, not really.'

'How long did it last?'

'Not long, a few minutes I suppose.'

'I'm worried I'll only manage seconds, I'll just come straight away, I know I will.'

'Isn't there anything you can do to slow it down?'

'They say if you think about something really boring that helps and you can keep going so that the girl gets to enjoy it as well.'

'Decide on something then, something from school, what's your worst thing?'

'*The Mill on the Floss.*'

'That's it then, think about *The Mill on the Floss.*'

Previously my only real intelligence or impression of sex

had come from Lin. With her there had seemed to be something abrasive and belligerent about it, some urging demand to be discharged, an itch to be rubbed. Talking to Julian about sex made it desirable but also funny, thus it was no longer frightening or excluding. About oral sex, however, I remained unconvinced. In the first form, when I was learning numbers in French, I asked Lin why she laughed when I got to soixante-neuf and she had drawn two tadpole-shaped people in the dust on our dressing-table mirror.

'He sucks hers and she sucks his.'

I thought it was disgusting. I asked Julian about it; he said that his friend Nick had had it done by a girl on the back seat of a coach.

'What about all the stuff, though?'

'What about it?'

'Do you have to swallow it? Can't you kind of hold it in your mouth and then spit it down the loo?'

Julian was particularly smitten with a woman who ran an Estée Lauder counter in one of the Knightsbridge department stores. He watched her going to work in the mornings in high white shoes and a corporate blue-patterned dress and gilt badge. One Saturday he pointed her out to me. She was, I guessed, in her late twenties, and very groomed. Privately I thought that he was being a little ambitious but, as his friend, I felt that I should be loyal and positive about his quest. She swayed in and out of his dreams each night in the bedroom that looked into the tree-tops of the park.

'What about you then, Susie, is there anyone you really want to sleep with? We could have a contest, to see who does it first.'

'Maybe.'

'Who is it? Is it the drummer? Boring if it is, every girl wants to sleep with him.'

'I don't.'

'All right then, older or younger than him?'

'Older, I suppose.'

'The stunt man, the one that looks like George Peppard?'

'No.'

'Not Barry, surely, he's too pissed all the time. And he probably wouldn't take his baker-boy cap off while he was doing it.'

Julian was mentally ticking off the habitués of the Chelsea Potter. When the shops on Kings Road closed many of the traders drifted to the Chelsea Potter pub on the corner of Radnor Walk. In those pre-punk days there was a lively community of customers who drank in pleasurable and discrete coexistence. Many trades and professions were represented there – the iron-monger from the shop next door, the rock drummer, the painter Barry French, fashion photographers, society hairdressers, the stunt man, a retired cat burglar, the editor of the *Chelsea Post*, a professional footballer, models and dancers and rogue knots of visiting businessmen who strayed in on trips from elsewhere, seeking chance thrills.

Julian and I, being the youngest, and strictly speaking having no place in a pub at all, were treated like pets. We remained unscathed by drugs although from time to time we drank adventurously. The Chelsea Potter was given to holding promotions for various drinks. On the Harvey Wallbanger night we were both insensible by eight o'clock. Julian's father took us home and covered us with blankets on the living-room floor.

'You look like the Babes in the Wood, for goodness' sake,' he said, next morning. Subsequently he lost his temper when he found that Julian had been sick on the bathroom floor; standing over us with a red plastic bucket he said, 'I ask you, is this any job for a man to be doing, is it honestly?'

An elderly American, known as Uncle Herm, was the

importer behind the second-hand clothing stock for the Jean Machine store further down the Kings Road. He was invariably magnanimous, clamping the end of his cigar in his mouth to free both arms to embrace us and plying us with drinks and the house food special which was a piece of steak sandwiched in a hunk of French bread. Julian said that he could not work out which of us Uncle Herm wanted to sleep with and then his mother, Lalla, commented that it was probably both of us, and simultaneously.

'Are you screwing Julian?' she asked me.

'Oh, please, don't,' said Julian, very embarrassed.

'No, I'm not actually, why?' I felt I should be combative to deflect from my friend's embarrassment.

'You surprise me; I thought you would be, little chickens.'

After that Lalla decided that she would take me up.

'You remind me so much of myself at your age, darling. I'm going to make you my protégée.'

Although I felt that Julian might be uneasy, at first I enjoyed being taken about by Lalla and I knew that I could learn from her what I sought to know. She said, 'I will teach you everything you need to know about men. You can have anyone you want, darling, anyone at all.'

'Even if it's wrong?'

'Wrong, what's wrong? There is no wrong, it's whether you want to or not, that's all that matters.'

Obediently I followed in the wake of her perfume; we went to the Village Club, which was a small private casino in Sloane Street, and to the Aretusa, a club with cool white walls, newly built on Kings Road. During the day Lalla wore trousers of conker brown made especially for her by the leather craftsman in Great Gear; in the evenings she wore dresses of cheesecloth which floated, ribboned and embroidered, around her bare brown body beneath. 'I don't wear knickers,' she told me. 'What's the point, I can never find them again the morning after.' She also told me that she shaved away her pubic hair. 'It's so much nicer, darling, believe me.'

As far as I was concerned, my own part in the excursions I made with Lalla was perfectly innocent. I had neither the wish nor the intention to go to bed with any of the men we attracted, those who sent us over cocktails in the Aretusa Club or gave us stacks of gambling counters at the Village gaming tables. It was fun and it was amusing, we ate choice suppers and we were cosseted by the staff of the establishments because we were an attraction and therefore good for business. There was ceremony to our entrances, the doorman would hold the door for us and Lalla would sashay through the lobby and heads would turn. I would follow like an acolyte. We never paid for drinks ourselves; sometimes champagne was sent across, sometimes concoctions in frosted glasses would arrive, the rims rimed with a stripe of frozen sugar and a strawberry to dip.

Reclining in her seat and with a starlet smile at her surroundings Lalla told me, 'It's all done with the eyes, darling, you don't need words at all. Go on, now you try.'

She, in the main, did have the wish and the intention to sleep with a number of the men that we ensnared. Sometimes there could be awkwardness when she was willing to go back to a flat or a hotel suite and I was not, leaving one disconsolate man in the party. One night, outside the Royal Court Theatre, a man who had bought us champagne shouted 'prick teaser' right into my face. On another evening I slipped away into the pavement shadows of Park Lane while we waited for a taxi; an American who made films said we were going to have threesomes, four-somes and anything you like-somes.

There were men with whom Lalla seemed to have an ongoing

but open arrangement. I knew that sometimes, during a slow afternoon's trading, she and Jimmy went into one of her changing booths together through the louvre doors like a saloon bar in a Western. Jimmy said he was content so long as he had one orgasm per day. Another of Lalla's regular men was a retired cat burglar, an Irishman who was nicknamed Scottie; he was lionised in some newspapers as the man who had stolen the jewels of an Italian film star. Sometimes he would call in to the market to see Lalla; he was a tall strong man with iron grey curls and blue eyes. During the day he wore cashmere jumpers which might be holey, the sleeves rolled up to his elbows, and gypsy-ish dark serge trousers. His platinum wrist watch was precious and thin as a wafer. Sometimes we encountered him on the evening excursions and then he would be very differently dressed, in a maroon velvet dinner jacket and a fancy frilled shirt. I liked his day clothes better.

One night Lalla was irritable, with a headache. Unusually, mild Peter had come into the market to remonstrate with her over some bills and some recent instances of behaviour.

'You don't own me,' she shouted at him, and then, 'I'm going to take Julian out for his supper. I suppose you will say you can't afford to feed him, you cheese-paring cunt.'

She had taken us to Finch's restaurant in the Fulham Road; she said that we must eat but that she wanted nothing because Peter had caused her to have a headache. A man at another table sent me a note on a sheet begged from a waiter's pad. It said, simply, 'I want to fuck you.' I giggled and showed it to Julian but Lalla snatched it from him and read it.

'I'm bloody sick of this,' she said bitterly, 'I've taught you too well, my girl, too many of my own tricks. You're pulling more than I am now.'

She was very annoyed with me. At first I did not realise that she was serious, her anger seemed stagey, the kind of acting she might once have done with a tight bodice and a beauty spot.

Just then Scottie the jewel thief arrived, parking his Jaguar arrogantly slewed to the kerb outside. He came in with expansive gestures and said that he would just have Apollinaris water as he was thinking of getting into training again. Rubbing his hands together, he said, 'Well, what have we here then,' and taking the seat at my side, he began to pay court to me. Lalla picked up my glass and snapped the bowl off the stem.

Scottie looked confused. 'Oh, now look here,' he began; Julian ushered me outside.

'She gets like that sometimes, don't worry about it.'

The following Saturday Lalla seemed to have forgotten. 'Julian is away with Peter this weekend. You and I will have special fun tonight.'

When Great Gear closed she said she would take me to meet a man called Tam Noble at a wine bar in Beauchamp Place. He too had been an actor; he spoke every sentence as if it was Shakespeare on a stage with poor acoustics. He wore a fedora and a belted overcoat of herringbone tweed. His eyelashes were the type that curl markedly upwards, and I thought that they might also have been mascara-ed. Lalla ordered me a large glass of sweet Spanish wine.

'This is my little friend, Susie, that I was telling you about. Susie, say hello to Tam. Tam, isn't she lovely? I thought we might have a little party.'

'A party, oh what delights.'

At the next table was a group of work colleagues celebrating a leaving ceremony for one of their number. Their gathering was noisy and good-humoured and they looked normal and ordinary.

Tam said, 'Shall I telephone for reinforcements? There's

some I know that wouldn't want to miss...' He stood up to find the payphone, oblivious that the skirt of his voluminous tweed coat brushed the bottles and glasses at the next table. One of the company put out his arms to prevent them falling. As he did so, I caught him exchanging glances and raised eyebrows with a colleague over the weirdness of Tam's appearance and his diction.

'Drink up, darling, then Lalla will buy you another.'

But there was not time. Tam returned, 'All arranged, the gang's all here.' He bent towards me, the beak of his nose was pronounced under the tilted brim of his hat,

'I live in Draycott Avenue, not far.' Tam's flat was a room where daylight seemed never to enter. It was not even possible to gauge whether and where there were windows behind the heavy velvet hangings which bowed the brass café rods. Everywhere there were such draperies, on walls and chairs and over a chaise longue. The fabrics were a mixture of heavy velvets and brocades, the sort of exotic, rich materials used to make cloaks for the three kings in Nativity plays.

'Drinks, I think,' said Tam.

I noticed that on a side table there was a bottle of Johnson's Baby Oil, its clean modern plastic lines incongruous amid the heaped and dusty faded materials.

'I'm going to the bathroom, darlings,' said Lalla.

Tam had poured me a glass of green Chartreuse.

'Would you care to see some photographs?' He produced a sheaf from the drawer of a shrouded side table. 'Do look.'

The top image was of a group of people standing around as if chatting at some social gathering. Their necks and faces were not included in the shot. All were clothed except for a man who had loosed his trousers to his knees and was pointing his very large erect penis towards the bottom of a woman who had lifted her skirt.

45

'Don't you like that one? Try another, little girl.' Tam's voice wheedled.

The next photograph was of two men, one sitting on the lap of the other, both were trouser-less but had retained their shirts and ties. A group of people, who may have been the same ones, stood in a circle around them as though it were a wrestling contest in a small sporting arena. I noticed that the light shone on the round spectacles on the upturned face of the man on the lap. Perhaps Tam noticed it too for he said, 'Flash bulbs, I must make sure to find them out.'

Lalla returned from the bathroom, smiling, her hair and make-up freshly done. From somewhere beyond the muffled room we heard a taxi stopping in the street below.

'Might be George, our first party guest, do hope so.'

'Oh, me too, darling,' replied Lalla, shrugging her shoulders and smiling in delight. It felt like school to me, the times when you sense the dislike that others have towards you, knowing that they are discussing and plotting though all the while they turn towards you friendly faces.

'I'm going to the bathroom too,' I said.

The bathroom was beside the front door. I heard the person who must be George being admitted although his voice was no more than urgent muttering in comparison to Tam's. On a shelf there were many old boxes of colognes and medical preparations, all covered with thick white fluffy dust. I heard Lalla greet George and then I opened the door and ran from the flat and from the building; out in the street I dodged behind cars, knowing that it must look ludicrous, like a television detective series. I had not felt fear until I allowed myself to start running; Tam's voice sounded from the doorway of the building, 'The bitch! The bitch has gone! Come here, bitch, come here!'

Further along the street I saw that there was a police panda car but I envisaged with what contempt a policeman would regard me if I stopped him and told my story.

I no longer heard Tam's voice at my back but even so I took a circuitous route, in and out of the narrow mews and around Chelsea Green before I returned to Kings Road. I found a small supermarket still open and went in and bought a bar of Cadbury's chocolate; the packaging was familiar but the writing was Arabic. I finished the bar as I reached Oakley Street. It was empty and quiet and my footsteps were soft as I passed my father's house. At the corner turning for Phene Street I looked up at the street lamps and the stars in the night sky; the gable end of the cream-painted terrace resembled a superior doll's house. I stood watching and I wished that smoke would issue gently from one of the chimney pots.

Julian appeared quite glad of the rift between Lalla and me. Although he did not say so, I guessed that since early childhood he had been frequently embarrassed by his mother's activities and by the humiliations to his father. In public he was never allowed to acknowledge Lalla as his mother, she insisted that he always called her by her first name.

On the afternoon of the last day of the spring term we were discussing our revision plans in the Picasso and then Julian said, 'Let's go to a pub somewhere that she won't be.'

We walked through the chilly evening air to the Phene Arms. The Phene was a pub with a quiet evening trade, predominantly male and local. Julian and I were conspicuous among its regulars and I wondered if we might not be served, because of our age. I was about to suggest to Julian that we moved on but then I saw the man sitting alone, sideways on to the bar. Over his shirt he wore a baggy jersey of navy blue and he was reading a newspaper. It was my father. For some moments it seemed impossible that the quiet contented company in their low-pitched conversation would remain oblivious to the blood rush and cacophony crashing inside me. I felt sure that their faces would turn in unison to watch me, as though I were making my entrance upon a theatre stage, and no certainty of either sympathy or applause from them.

Julian went to the bar and I looked for a table. I thought that my gait might stagger as I moved but I made sure to find a place where I could sit directly in my father's line of sight. Julian was waiting for the barman to fetch change. I sat down on the upholstered bench and pressed my back and knees against the cushions to prevent the shaking. After a few moments I had the courage to look about me and be assured that, extraordinary as it might seem, no one had guessed what was going on inside me. By the time Julian came to sit down I was calm, I tasted the floweriness of the cold wine and I recalled, by rote, what Lalla had taught me about the use of the look, that to effect a connection with another person the eyes were all that were necessary.

Julian was much taken up with a conquest he had made the previous evening; in imparting and evaluating the encounter, he did not, for some time, notice my preoccupation. I was noting how thin was my father's face, the skin and muscles drawn so tight and spare across the bones that it reminded me of an anatomical poster in the science laboratory at school. It was not, however, thin in a way suggestive of ill health or hunger, but of discipline or self-denial. His skin was slightly tanned, not in a holiday colour, more like the complexion of a New Zealander. With age his eyes had become more deep set than in the photograph, the brows and eyebrows a little lower and more forward. At the front his dull blond hair was long; from time to time he pushed it back unconsciously with the flat of his hand as he leant over his newspaper. He was drinking beer. He called the barman by his first name and his shoes were battered brown but polished.

Gleefully, Julian was recounting how, on the evening before, he had met a girl in the darkness of the Pheasantry Club and she had mistaken him for the teen idol singer, David Cassidy.

'Did you tell her you weren't him?'

'Of course not. She was kissing me and everything. She wanted to go outside with me as well.'

I calculated that at any moment my father would finish the column he was reading and that then he would have to lift his head to turn the broadsheet page.

'Did you then?'

'No, I thought she might find out, under the street lights, that I wasn't him. I said that I couldn't take advantage of a fan. God, it nearly killed me not to. I wish I'd chanced it now.'

My father, lifting his head from the completed article, raised his eyes to turn the page and saw that I was staring. From that moment I knew that he was mine.

'Are you listening?' Julian asked me, while my father, somewhat discountenanced, made a poor job of folding over the thick sheets.

'Yes, you wish that you had done stuff after all. Didn't she wonder why you were there on your own?'

'No, because Jimmy from Great Gear was in there so I got him to pretend to be my manager. He came across with drinks for us. I'll have to pay him back on Saturday.'

There was a nerve or muscle in my father's cheek that twitched periodically. I waited for him to look over a second time; he would need to see whether his eyes had deceived him on the first occasion. I was quite ready for him when he did; outwardly most cool, though under my ribs there was a sensation like a press stud closing as our eyes met. Everything that I sought was contained there, all the world in that brief connection made across the saloon bar space.

'So, did you get her phone number?'

'Yes, but I can't arrange to see her, not in daylight.'

'She might go back there tonight, to look for you. I would, if I were her.'

Julian's small boy's small round eyes widened with delight as he appraised this prospect.

My father asked Sylvester the barman for another drink. He stood up to reach change from his pocket. Once more it made me want to weep as I watched because each move and attitude of his body was beloved and just as I had always imagined it would be.

'Are you trying to pull that guy at the bar?'

Julian was curious but not in the least dismayed. After all, he had witnessed the transaction of many of his own mother's liaisons; in age Lalla's partners had ranged from the septuagenarian to a boy from the sixth form at Julian's school, the latter episode taking place during the tea interval of the leavers' cricket match. Such comrades in the pursuit of the desired were we, Julian and I, that immediately he rose saying, 'Look, I'll go to the Gents to give you some more room. Don't worry, I'll take my time.'

And, as if by some serendipitous stage direction, other customers began to drift homewards. Twice the well-oiled door with its frosted glass panel swung to the cold Chelsea evening beyond. Twice too Jack smiled at me.

Julian reappeared animated by eager purpose, his hair newly combed and a few coins jingling in his palm. 'So, how's it going?' he nodded with an import of innuendo and the feathery strands at the crown of his head trembled.

'Good, it's good.'

'Okay, well, I don't expect she will, because she has to get a train from Reading and stuff, but just in case, I think I will wander up to the Pheasantry and see. I've got just enough to pay us both in if you like...'

'No, I think I'll stay.'

'On your own, really?'

'I'll be okay.'

'You look amazing tonight, Suse, be careful, won't you.'

Julian left and I followed him in my mind's eye, walking brisk and cheerful and full of hope towards the Kings Road, still jingling the coins in his palm.

Somewhere in another part of the Phene Arms a telephone began to ring. 'I'll need to go,' said Sylvester, apologetically. 'They're all away out.'

Then we were the only two left in the bar. Jack stood up and began to walk towards me. Although it was but a distance of fifteen feet or so, the leaf-patterned carpet seemed like the void that must be crossed in dreamscapes; I willed him not to falter.

'Er, has he gone... your...' he gestured to the place where Julian had sat.

'Yes, he has. He's my friend, a sort of brother, but not.'

'Okay, I see, sort of, but not... would you mind if I...'

Of the two of us, we both knew that he was the one who was shy and awkward. 'Listen,' he was moving his fingers down the surface of his glass as if he were sculpting it from clay, 'I couldn't help noticing... noticing that you were looking over, and so on, just now. To be honest, I've been wondering if you thought I was someone else, somebody you knew...'

I smiled at him properly for the first time because I wanted to reassure him, 'No, I didn't think you were anyone else.'

'Oh, okay. Well, my name is Jack, by the way.'

'Jack.' I had repeated it many times over in my head as I tried out his mouth and traced imaginary contacts with his imagined body. Never, until then, had I spoken it out loud.

'Yes, and may I... may I know your name?'

'My name is Susie. Susanna, but people call me Susie.'

'And, do you live around here, Susie?'

'No, I live across the river.' I did not dare to say Clapham. In my head I conjured Julian's flat in the red-brick mansions facing the park, 'In Prince of Wales Drive.'

'Ah yes, I know it.'

He lifted his arm to drink. I saw that the veins on the back of his hands stood out in relief, that there were a few freckles and golden hairs there and on his wrists. The glass of his watch was scratched and he wore it on a fabric strap of navy blue and red. When he looked at me, only an arm's length from myself, and I saw how nervous he was, I wanted to tell him there and then how much I loved him and to let my head fall like a dead weight on his chest and to be done with all pretending.

I did not, of course. I sat silent, adjusting myself to the emotion which I felt for my father beside me. It was a physical phenomenon; there was some tidal rise in the circulation of my blood. If I could have looked under my clothes I expected that my chest would have been suffused with a flush, like cochineal dripped into white icing.

Sylvester the barman, sensing the musk on the air, folded a towel and retreated through the archway to the public bar.

'Show me where you live,' I said, holding my father in my gaze.

Jack was caught off guard. He enunciated one or two of the phonic forms to which Englishmen resort when they are embarrassed or require a moment to collect their thoughts, then, 'Are you propositioning me?'

He gave a half smile but I did not smile at him at all. Instead

I continued to stare at him full face with the look akin to inso-lence that gamblers use to regard their opponents in games of chance.

'Listen.' Jack stood up and pushed back his hair; the muscle in his left cheek twitched. 'Listen, I'm not quite sure what's going on here...'

Sylvester faltered, hesitating like a prompt in the wings lest we should require another round.

I stood up too. 'Let us go,' I said.

Outside in Phene Street I took his arm in such a way that he could be aware of the softness of my cheek and upper arm and breast against him but he gave no sign of response. He was too intent on walking, stalking almost, straight and stiff and upright. Neither did it occur to him that I seemed to know the way. We stopped outside number 33 Oakley Street.

'I could... I could make you a cup of coffee.'

'That would be very nice.'

He laughed, 'God help me, first you pick me up, and now you're going all demure on me.' In the hall my father said, 'Come here, Miss, the timer for the lights goes out and leaves you in the pitch black unless you sprint. I'll take your hand.'

Ascending the three dark flights, it was an act of supreme self-denial, now that I had his hand in mine at last, not to take up his long fingers and try them inside my mouth, one by one, to see whether they tasted salty against the pink of cheek flesh.

'Well, here it is.' He pushed open the door. 'It's a bit bare, I'm afraid. A bit like a monk's cell I suppose, but I'm only here during the week, mostly. At weekends I go back to Suffolk.'

I knew that to mean that he had a wife there. 'Do you have children?' My question came out sounding rude and clipped because of the fury I might have to suppress against his possible answer.

'You're very direct, aren't you, for one so young. No, I don't, as a matter of fact. Why do you ask?'

'Just wondered.'

'I did have, a long, long time ago. They're on the other side of the world now... they emigrated with their mother when they were tiny things.'

There was a curtained-off kitchen section to the room. He went in there to boil a red enamel coffee pot. I looked around my father's room and willed my eyes and memory to work like a spy's microfilm camera.

The green curtains were drawn over the window which looked down on Phene Street. In front of the window there was a big light oak desk with solid Art Deco-shaped handles to the drawers. On this desk there was a homemade stand of roughish wood, like a lectern, but with the slope at an angle less acute. Beside the stand, in rows, were stoneware marmalade jars holding pens and brushes; there were bottles of inks, a black metal watercolour box and a cloisonné bowl of Chinese ink sticks. Everywhere it was extremely neat and functional: a record player, a stack of LPs, bookshelves with postcard reproductions of Paul Nash and Stanley Spencer paintings propped against the spines.

There was an armchair and an upright chair for the painting desk. I sat on the bed; it was narrow and had a cover of snuff-coloured crêpe de Chine.

'Sugar?' my father asked. I shook my head with nonchalance although my heart had skipped beats when I realised that he had been standing watching me.

He brought the coffee cups. 'I am an illustrator,' he explained, nodding towards the desk. 'I do books and magazine work, that sort of thing.'

He sat in the armchair. I focused on the coffee in my cup

yet all the time I felt that he was observing me and it was as though he was covering me with gold or some other precious substance.

'Why me?' he asked, after a while; his tone was stern.

'What do you mean?'

'I mean why me, why did you pick on me to...' He opened out his hands to finish the sentence with a gesture, and then, 'Things like this don't just happen... not to me, anyway... not nowadays...'

'They do, sometimes they do.'

'But why should it happen, why there and then and why to me?'

'Why not?'

I knew that it was a contest but that it was a safe one, of the parlour game kind. I knew too that I must only maintain my conviction to keep trumping him every time.

'Why not... I'll tell you why not, Susie, shall I? Here am I, I'm over fifty, for God's sake, and you, how old are you?'

'Eighteen.' I said it with neither a blink nor a flinch.

'Eighteen, Susie, for heaven's sake, look at you, with your long, long hair and your big brown eyes... you do know, do you, that you have what are commonly known as come-to-bed eyes... you couldn't not, I suppose. Look, you are... you are an exceptionally lovely young woman. I am an older, old if you like, man.'

I sat and watched my father's face; it was the only thing in the world that I wanted to see.

'You're doing it again, for Christ's sake, Susie... Listen, I will tell you about me... I am fifty-two, I have a wife and a house in Suffolk where I spend my weekends doing middle-aged things like making an asparagus bed. I am not rich, I am a vaguely successful jobbing artist. I drive a 1962 Citroën which makes odd noises on the motorway... There is nothing about me that could possibly appeal to... someone... someone like you, Susie...'

His voice, in general deep and the words each considered, had risen slightly in the plaint of his self-deprecation. Also, perhaps, because he had told a lie about his age.

'Tonight, like any other night, I go for a quiet drink in what is possibly the dullest pub in London... and then you, you appear. I really don't understand.'

'I wanted to. I like you.'

He made a sound and a gesture indicative of despair as though I had given him an answer that disappointed him. I knew, in fact, that it was quite the opposite. I looked at his battered brown shoes and his trousers of fine cord and the way in which one hand held the coffee cup on his knee.

'Can I give you a lift somewhere, drive you home or something?'

'No, it's okay, I'll get a taxi.'

'Are you sure?'

'Certain sure.' I smiled at him and he smiled back at me.

All the way down the stairs and along the hall he held my hand. I felt that I could draw him into me by the arm, as though on a string of coloured yarn.

We stood on the doorstep. You could tell that the sea was in the air from the river. The pillars on the porticoes of the houses in Oakley Street are fairly grand. Beside them even my tall father seemed on a more human scale. It was incredible to me that nearby, in Kings Road, people continued to do ordinary evening things.

'Listen,' he said, 'listen, if, you know... in the cold light of day... if you really feel that you would like to come again, then I, then I would, of course, be very glad to see you... after all, how could I not be...' He touched my cheek with two of his fingers. I had to press my feet hard on to the stone step beneath me so that I should not gasp out loud.

'Good night, little one,' Jack said.

For some way I did not even try to find a taxi. At Cheyne Walk I turned left and crossed to the embankment side. I wished to walk slowly and more than once I know that I smiled at the night. I wanted also to be close beside the river. At that date, if you grew up and went to school in south London, you seemed, somehow, to be related to the Thames. It was a constant and familiar presence in your consciousness; you crossed it for excursions and railway termini and the Christmas lights, you knew it from the avuncular narratives of history textbooks.

Over Chelsea Bridge I walked tall when the bikers at the teastall whistled and gestured obscenities. At the bank corner in Queenstown Road stood the Irish boys; Alison had told me fearful tales of their gang and what they did and yet they caused me no alarm. I felt that I was protected by some radiance from any insult. Eventually I found a taxi and it drove me swiftly home across the Avenue on Clapham Common. Then I could lie down and make believe that the pillow against my cheek was the fingers of my father's hand.

The next day was the beginning of that time when I saw the world in a different way. It was not a very long time, in terms of life spans, but while it lasted it was very good and very vivid. I remember that I noticed, especially, the colour of things. In old post-war guidebooks for Paris there are photographs of the flower markets; the blooms are exquisitely bright against the grey and wearied city. That is how I saw London in 1972. Details and people mattered; all of their stories counted because each of them was a component part in the days when I would see my father, or in the days when I was waiting to see him and counting and crossing off hours on the end page of a book or the edge of a paper bag. Every feature of a scene was clear and true, as though my eyes depicted the world for me in *plein air*.

In the morning the tall Austrian manageress was unlocking the metal shutter blind of the American Dream, trying to keep her head straight and level as she bent towards the pavement. 'Thank God. Thank God you're here, my hangover is the end.'

She sat in the window at the table where the varnish always looked sticky and asked me to put the coffee machine on without bothering to clean it. She smoked a number of cigarettes which she stood up on their filter end when she had finished, letting them burn out rather than looking for an ashtray.

'It's my boyfriend,' she explained when I brought her black coffee. 'We are finished but we can't leave each other alone.'

Renata winced when Ali the chef banged through the door, his immense height accentuated by his inevitable companion, the little old man in a beret who was the washer-up. The little man worked in rubber gloves which extended past his elbows; he seemed to speak no English. Ali spoke only a little; Renata said that he knew all the wrong words. His moods transformed with rapidity, from anger to lechery, from melancholy to a loud, singing cheerfulness. At this moment he was already furious, prowling around the stainless-steel kitchen in clog shoes and shaking his black curls. 'Hey, you twos,' he called us through the hatch, 'you, bloody shits delivery don't come, bloody shits.'

His voice was very deep and rolling; he pronounced bloody as if there were one o and two ds. I looked over at the clock which told the time with Coca Cola bottle hands, calculating the hours until I could revisit my father's room. Ali muttered and swiped at the prep table with a cleaver. The little man, who seemed sometimes to assume the role of a placatory, long-suffering spouse, tuned in their radio. A Neil Young song was playing. Ali began to hum along with it,

> *When you were young and on your own,*
> *how did it feel to be alone...*
> *Only love can break your heart...*
> *yes only love can break your heart...*

Then he slopped back to the hatch and rested his elbows there, tweaking at hairs in his beard and rolling his eyes at me in a grotesque pantomime parody of seduction.

'You want to come in the alley with me, sugar pie?'

'No.' I was pairing knives and forks in red paper napkins.

'I'm hot sex,' he insisted, 'real hot Ali.'

'I don't want to, thank you.' I shook my head over the cutlery. Mireille, the French waitress, arrived. She wore a scarlet cheese-cloth smock without a bra beneath it. Her prim brown bobbed hair framed her face all of a piece.

'Hey, Mireille, you don't want to come in Ali's alley, do you?' He turned back to me. 'Mireille don't want to, she is lez. You is lez, ain't you, honey?'

'Fuck off,' said Mireille, swinging her Milly-Molly-Mandy bob.

'Fuck off you self,' returned Ali, 'bloody fucks to you.'

The restaurant was very busy and our apron pockets were weighed down with tips which we were not allowed to change in the till. At my break Ali, unexpectedly, brought me a plate loaded with all the specials from the menu. 'You eat,' he said, banging the plate down.

I looked at him questioningly.

'You have a man now, you have to eat. Men like, you know, big all over. You know it's the truth.' He nodded to affirm his message.

*

At the end of the shift I washed away the restaurant smells in the staff shower. My hair was still damp when I walked down Kings Road and my scalp felt the chill edge to the air. The scent I used in those days was Diorissimo, it was like lily of the valley.

Jack's writing on the card for the bell push was black italic. He was wearing the same navy blue jersey and he looked at me with a kind of reproof. 'So, you came back then.'

Up in his room his manner was at first pedagogic, as though he must instruct me in the complicated parts of some theorem. 'Listen, Susie, I've been thinking about this a lot since last night, well, all the time, actually...'

He moved his thoughts along with his hands; the leaves and plantlets of the spider plant on the window sill trembled slightly at the disturbance.

'I think I have to tell you, first, about me, and then you decide... whether you really want to keep coming to see me. You know that I really don't have anything to offer you... I am married, permanently, I suppose you could say. I've not been unfaithful, at all, before, to Olive – that's my wife. Years ago, it was a different story, I was a different man... I behaved in ways that I am not proud of; I let people down, all sorts of people. Then, and it served me right, I got myself into a mess, I was drinking too much, I couldn't work, it all sort of caught up with me. Then I met Olive and she... she's solid, she helped me sort myself out. We got married and we have made a life together. It might not be a very exciting life, or what I once expected, but it's what I can cope with. I can make a decent job of it. I owe Olive a great deal. I wouldn't, ever, want to hurt her.'

'Where did you meet?'

'At Kingston, at Kingston School of Art, I taught a course

there and she... she teaches there too, enamelling.'

My eyes were so big and so dark, then. It was easy to make them look as if I was about to cry.

'Look, Susie, look... what I suppose I am trying to say to you is that you, you are such a lovely young woman, I am immensely flattered... God, there must be young men queuing halfway to Sloane Square for you, I should think... But me, what could I possibly have to give you...'

I stood up and went to look through the window onto Phene Street. I think Jack feared that he had managed after all to persuade me and that I was about to turn away and leave him. For a little while I watched the pub dog, grubbing and questing at the garden hedge. And then I stepped forward and kissed my father on his lovely mouth.

I know that Jack was going back to Suffolk for the Easter weekend. I wondered what Olive looked like, but only in a disconnected, idle way, as I might have done on hearing that a new teacher was coming to the school. There was never any question that I should feel jealous of her. Neither did it occur to me that she should have any bearing on my relationship to my father. In loving Jack I was a zealot; there was no other point of view, no other belief system but mine.

In the Great Gear Trading Company somebody dropped a wallet. Julian picked it up and brought it behind the stall that I was watching. We ate a bag of marshmallows and wondered what we ought to do. Eventually Julian suggested that we should look inside first, before deciding.

'Fuck me,' he said, as it opened onto a substantial quantity of notes. We thought that we had better hand it in but then Julian remembered that he had an invitation to a party at the home of

a girl in Weybridge. 'I never thought I'd be able to go, but look...
I can buy drink and things... you can come too. Her parents are
away and everything. Her dad's an accountant and he looks
after all sorts of people, there might be pop stars.'

'No, I don't think I will.'

Julian knew that in other days the prospect would have held
great appeal for me. 'But look, we can both get something really
good to wear out of this...'

'No, really.'

He was surprised and also annoyed at my refusal. Not, I knew,
for the sake of my company especially, but because he was nervy
at the prospect of performing should sex arise and he wanted my
conspiratorial reassurance that he would be good at it.

'If you're going to be like that I won't bother.' He picked at
the bottom of his shoe, which was blue with a narrow platform
in a lighter shade. 'Why are you being such a downer anyway,
it's really anti-social.'

After some minutes of ignoring each other, Julian suddenly
grinned. 'I know, you crafty... you've got someone, haven't you?
Who is it, is it someone from the Potter? If it's Scottie you do
know that my mother will kill you, don't you?'

I smiled but said nothing.

'I'll find out. I will, I can promise you that.' Then he bent
down under the chipboard counter and divided the cash
into two equal sums for us. I went out and spent all mine on
a silk shirt. I bought it from a black and silver shop owned by
a former model and her photographer. He still took pictures
of her, manipulating the images of her body into surreal
zippered shapes suspended on coat hangers; there were poster-
size reproductions for sale. I was entranced by my shirt, by its
costliness despite its exceptional plainness. It was the colour
of vanilla ice cream and made from raw silk so that when you

touched it you felt that the pads of your fingers might adhere.

When the market closed Julian's harassed father, Peter, arrived to drive him down to Surrey. In Oakley Street some women were unloading armfuls of flowers from the back of a car to decorate the church of Our Most Holy Redeemer and St Thomas More for Easter Day. One had a basket filled with yellow narcissus and blue hyacinth. The fragrance was so strong that it stayed suspended on the air for some time after she had gone.

On Easter Sunday morning Ron went out early to deliver chocolate eggs to his children.

'There's one for you there, if you want it,' my mother said. In her mauve quilted dressing gown she had appeared to collect a tea tray and the *Sunday Express* to take back to bed. 'We're driving out somewhere later, Box Hill, probably. Ron might pick up his dogs, to give them a proper run, seeing as she never takes them out for a walk. You don't want to come, do you?'

'No, thank you.'

'I don't know when we'll be back, we shan't rush.'

'I might stay at Alison's.' I had never mentioned the family's remove to the estate on the old Croydon airfield.

'Please yourself. I doubt that Lin will be home, she'll probably help out down at the pub, now that she's up and about again.'

My sister had spent some days in bed, following the termination of her pregnancy. She and my mother seemed to discount the matter. Because I found it upsetting I put away contemplation of it in a section of my mind that I could shut off. When they discussed the operation I used only part of my conscious awareness, in the same way as you can prevent yourself from breathing in a bad smell.

I supposed that my sister's requirement for an abortion had

made it easier for me to obtain the contraceptive pill from the elderly GP. Without question he had scrawled me an introduction to the family planning clinic on a slip of yellow paper. Lin's introduction to the women's surgical he had scrawled on a slip of green paper. It was all the same hospital, opposite the tube station at Clapham South.

When the flat was empty I spent a long time making myself ready for my father. I knew that I looked very beautiful, apart from my fingernails. I was never adept at painting the nails of my right hand. I smudged them and went over the edges. I searched for remover among Lin's things but found none. I looked at my hands critically as I walked towards the bus stop. There were families coming home from the Common. Little girls with white cardigans buttoned over their dresses. The afternoon was grey and it looked as if it would rain.

In Oakley Street Jack's car was already back, like a huge shell beside the kerb. The rain had begun, soft and fine. When he opened the door and I first met his eyes on the threshold I was filled with awe at what I had done and at what I was about to do. We sat down opposite each other, me on the bed, and him on the armchair.

'I don't know, Susie, what are we going to do with you?' He watched my face while I did not answer. 'The thing is... I'm trying to be fair, to both of us. I'm not sure that you know what you want.'

'I do.'

'Do you, I wonder. By the way, I don't know whether the blouse... and... and everything is especially for my benefit, but if it is, I have noticed, and it's... it's very lovely.'

'I have the thing,' I said. Beside me was my handbag, a flat satchel of turquoise suede with mushroom shapes appliquéd to it. I took out the box of contraceptive pills and held it up to show him. 'It means ...'

'I know what it means.' He stayed still, staring at me. I was glad of the beautiful silk shirt, I knew that it would hold up well under his scrutiny. Suddenly he caught sight of my fingernails and leant forward to take up one of my hands.

'What have you been doing?' The excuse for action seemed quite to restore him.

'Show me – look at it, Susie – it's a mess.' He shook his head in indulgent despair.

'I know it's a mess.' One of my hands lay on one of his and I wanted to snap closed on it like an oyster shell and to mark his palms with my nails.

'Do you want me to sort it out for you?'

'Yes, please.'

He took a bottle from the painting desk and then manoeu-vred his chair close to me; his long thighs were either side of mine. In places of habitual creasing, at the groin and at the knees, the lines of the cord nap on his trousers had worn away, as corduroy does. He tipped solution from the bottle onto small pieces of lint and began to clean each nail meticulously. It stung a little between the skin and the nail bed. His hair fell forward as he worked. More than once I saw the muscle twitch in his cheek. He continued in silent concentration and careful method until each nail was done.

'There,' he held out my hand to admire his work. I saw that against his hand mine still seemed as podgy as it had been at primary school when we had made patterns by drawing around our fingers.

'Do you want me to re-do them for you?' He looked up at me as he asked. I only nodded, for my voice was gone. He himself was quite gruff. 'All right, give me the stuff then.'

I found the bulbous little Mary Quant bottle in my bag. His eyes remained downcast as he spread my fingers and began to paint. I saw that the brushstrokes were deft and deliberate, using very little varnish. When he had finished the first coat he lifted my hands and supported them in the air upon his as if it were the preliminary to some courtly dance. Then he blew on each finger end to help them to dry. When he painted the last nail for the second time I thought that my heart might burst out through my ears or throat.

'There,' he said, and placed my hands upon his knees. We both looked down at them; he rested his forehead against my bowed head. Slowly and deliberately, as though I were his pupil or his witness he asked me, 'Do you know what's going to happen now?'

I replied yes but the end was missing from my word.

'And do you want it to happen, Susanna? Is it really what you want?'

I said yes again but I spoke the sound inside his mouth.

The bed was so narrow that all through the night, even when I was deeply asleep, I knew that Jack was very close beside me. I awoke in the morning because he was going in to me again.

'I cannot believe how soft your skin is.' He was looking closely at a small area of my shoulder, inspecting it as experts examine sections of paint and pigment to date canvases. I heard footsteps on the landing outside, walking softly, but with a heavy tread.

'It's all right, it's only Eunice, she lives upstairs. Kiss me like that again.'

Later when I was dressing he stood in the middle of the room with bare feet and no shirt. It could have been a holiday house and us off outside to stroll on the beach and to pick up shells and him pointing out the hidden primitive creatures in rock pools to make me squeal.

'Listen, Miss, I still think I should drive you home, I feel I should insist.'

'It's all right, really.'

'Well, I don't know, I'm a bit out of touch, of course, but surely it's still... I mean when you've spent the night with a man isn't it usual for him to make some effort to take you home?'

I was buttoning up the shirt; it had fine wrinkles at the arms and at the waist, like a shed skin. 'I've no idea.'

'What do you mean, no idea?'

'I mean I wouldn't know, whether they do or not.' I stood up to find my shoes.

'Now, hold on a minute, Susie, I think I need to ask you something.'

I knew what it was going to be.

'Susie, you have done this before, with a man, haven't you?'

'No, you are the first.'

I was glad that I had decided that the Windmill Drive occasion did not count. How sweet it was to provoke his reaction. At first he had to resort to the phonic forms again and he shook his head and pushed back his hair where it fell forward.

'Susie, I really don't think I know what to say to that... I mean, I did wonder but I... I never thought... Come here, you.'

My father held open his arms for me and when I was inside he put them around me and then crossed them over, behind my back, so that I was doubly held and protected. He rubbed his face in my hair and breathed in it and sighed into it and then he said, 'So, will you come and see me again?'

'Can I come tonight?'

'Of course you can. You must come whenever you like. I'll always be here. But listen, Susie,' he took my head in his two hands and held my face to look at me, 'when you feel, you know, when you decide that you want to stop coming, then that's all right too, know that it is all right, when it happens.'

'It won't happen.'

'It might do.'

'It won't.' I kissed him again.

On the way home I discovered that while sometimes semen runs back out of you straight away, at other times it stays inside you for ages. You are unaware until it comes out in a sudden rush; you can feel a certain alarm at this unexpected leak. After the shock of it, walking home across the Common from Cedars Road, it was amusing. Also, the utter secrecy of the phenomenon, even in the most public of settings, appealed to me. I contemplated how many of the stories that we tell ourselves are crafted from secrets. It begins with fairy tales: the sleeping enchanted are hidden away behind many layers of concealment. Chamber, tower, castle, courtyard, drawbridge, thorn and forest.

In the kitchen I felt light-headed with hunger. When I reached for the cupboard I thought that the leak was going to happen again so I tried standing in a cross-legged attitude, like a ballet position. I cut bread and spooned golden syrup on to it from the tin, mesmerised by the gorgeous transparent colour as it fell and spiralled from the spoon.

'What the hell are you doing?' My mother had come in behind me.

'Nothing.'

I folded the bread and put it into my mouth and edged out of the room. I went to bed until it was time to get up for the shift at the restaurant. Sighing in and out of sleep, I recreated my father's arms and his body and the sound of his voice deep inside my ear in the dark night room. 'You cling like a limpet, don't you? No, don't stop, I don't mean that I want you to let go, it's just that I don't think anyone's ever held on to me so tightly before.'

From that time I took to staying with Jack on as many nights or part-nights as I dared. My mother raised no objections; I told her that I was staying with Alison. I embroidered, explaining that Alison's mother had taken a job in the evenings at a cinema box office so that we babysat the young brothers. I wondered if Alison would mind if she knew how much I used her in my deceits. She had written to me once; she had annotated the paper with small biro hearts when referring to boys. She said that she liked the high school she attended and that she had made friends with a girl whose father was an army major. Write back soon, she insisted, with many exclamation marks, in her closing line, but I did not because I knew that we had left each other behind.

I had also to be careful of Lin. All our lives, if she was not fully occupied she was likely to seek diversion in bullying me. Once when I came home from Jack at past midnight she was sitting alone in the living room.

'What the hell do you do till this time of night?' she asked.

'Oh, you know, just stuff.' I sat on the arm of a chair so that she would not think I was trying to get away from her. She lit a cigarette, there was only one left in her packet and the ashtray was full. I thought about the evening I had spent with our father. I had finished waitressing at seven o'clock and Jack had jazz playing on the record player. I sat cross-legged on the bed and he sat looking at me until the music finished. When someone loves you that much it is like feeling the sun on your face. The needle lifted off the record and Jack came over to the bed. When I knew that he was about to put his fingers on me or in me I could feel it and rehearse it happening before ever he made contact. Sitting on the chair arm in the living room I shook myself out of remembering what he had done before Lin noticed.

'How is Mickey?' I asked her. Mickey was the new boyfriend who ran his uncle's pub.

'Bastard hasn't rung me tonight, that's what I'm sitting up for.'

'Do you want me to keep you company?'

'No, it's okay, you get to bed, you've got school in the morning.'

In fact, we were being given time off from school to begin revising for our O levels. I did not tell them at home, instead I used the days to take on more shifts at the restaurant. During my breaks I would sit at one of the tables at the back and annotate my copy of *Richard II* and Ali would bring me plates of apple pie and ice cream.

When I stayed the whole night long with Jack I was sure that time passed differently in the room above Phene Street. It was not only because I wished it to have lasted longer than it did. It did not seem like ordinary time, measured by the movement of clocks, but as if it was being counted by some other device, like the fall of drops of water. When he pushed me very hard I thought that we ourselves must surely fall. Down through the floors of the tall house in Oakley Street and on, beyond and below, descending through the centuries of London layers until we reached the first clay that the river itself laid down.

I think I was quiet mostly, it was a shyness I still had, though all physical hesitation soon left me. Jack was not silent, sometimes his moans repeated on and on, like a singer who is practising scales.

At other times he talked to me incessantly, whispers all in nonsense endearments repeated into my ear that lulled and soothed me until the stage when he knew that I did not own myself any more. And each time he was persuading me in the dark of my inner ear, telling me, 'Now see, see what I can do to you, Susie, you can't help it, can you, there is nothing I can't make you do for me, nothing, now you really have to give yourself to me, don't you, now, now you are mine, now you are all mine.'

But each time he did not know that it was not only my succumbing to the seducer's braggadocio lullaby that meant that I belonged to him. Each time I was imprinted on my father and his history like the negatives that become overlaid, one image upon another, on the film of an old camera. By taking my hand he had joined me to him and to that history, to the lawns and terraces of the Edwardian summer gardens, to the formal, sad- eyed people and their raffish terrier dogs and to the pages in the clasped albums where all pressed flowers turn to the colour of straw.

In the early mornings while he moved around the room and the curtained kitchen and I waited to hear the gas jet light under the kettle, I would lie watching him at these domestic rituals as rapt as if he had been a priest preparing at the altar. He made tea in one big white cup which we shared. I learnt to like tea brewed strong, and with sugar, although I had not done before. Before we got up properly we would sit side by side in the bed, leaning against each other as though it was the end of a journey. We would hear Eunice moving around and talking in low tones to herself or to her cat. Quite early on Jack decided that he should explain my presence to her; I stayed in the room while he waylaid her on the landing.

'Eunice, I just thought I should mention it... you may have seen Susanna, Susie, she's a friend of mine, sometimes she stays the night.'

'I know, Jack, I've heard.'

I could tell that he was embarrassed, I heard him shuffle his feet in the battered brown shoes. 'Yes, well, I know what you're probably thinking, Eunice, that there's no fool like an old fool, but it's just... it's just happened, with Susie... all right, I know it can't last, but every day it goes on and I am with her is... it is a bonus.'

'There is nothing wrong with fools, Jack, let's have more of them, that's what I say.'

At first, because I was too young to identify her brusqueness as the exoskeleton of the irretrievably shy, I felt an uneasy dislike for Eunice. Later, when I discovered her innate kindness and perception, I recalled those first feelings of mine with guilt. Later still, in the end, I used to think of her deliberately, because it brought me the relief of tears.

In the beginning it was also her appearance that unsettled me. She wore dark serge suits and men's black lace-up shoes and her coarse hair was cut short and into the back of her head, in barber's fashion. Her exposed neck, in colouration and texture, reminded me of the slices of luncheon meat that my mother gave us with salad. Eunice worked in the accounts department of Peter Jones in Sloane Square. One or two evenings of the week she also had a job in a pub behind Cheyne Walk; Julian, meeting friends from school, had once strayed there by mistake. He had found it memorable on two counts, first because it was peopled entirely by women, all wearing men's suits, and secondly because they served him orange squash rather than orange juice with his vodka.

Eunice and my father shared the coat stand and the party- line telephone on the landing and the bathroom with its old hissing gas geyser and tin of Vim. Eunice kept a cat named Haddock. Haddock was pure black and rigid in hauteur towards everyone except my father. He sought out Jack's company, sitting sculpturally still and polished for hours on the painting desk while he worked. Periodically, although he was fond of him, Jack harangued the impassive cat. 'Look at the bloody thing, for God's sake, it's like something out of ancient Egypt. Move, you bastard.'

My birthday is the first of June. On the morning of my seventeenth birthday I was stuffing books into my schoolbag on top of the clothes that I needed for the afternoon shift at the restaurant and the houndstooth check of the Diorissimo box. I used to leave my uniform in the school cloakroom. The week before I had been threatened with a detention because someone had stolen my tie and so I had to wait until a games lesson and steal another girl's. A detention would have made me late for crossing the river.

Fixed as I was upon the bag stuffing, I was startled when Ron looked into the room and unexpectedly announced, 'Many happy returns.'

I heard him saying something quietly to my mother in the kitchen and then her voice rose in disgruntled response, 'Well, she said she didn't want any fuss. I didn't bloody know, did I?'

'But surely, Mo, a bit of something, a cake and that...'

'We're not that sort of family.'

She came into the room. 'Well, do you want us to do any-thing special tonight, seeing as it's your birthday? Do you want us to take you out for a drink?'

With her expression she was defying me to say that I did wish for some effort to be made. It occurred to me that my sister might have played out the situation like the line on a fishing reel.

'No, that's fine. I'll be staying over at Alison's.'

She bustled to fetch her purse. 'Here, I wasn't just going to do nothing.' She handed me a note but she was looking at Ron.

'And here's a little one from me,' he said, also handing me money.

After the restaurant shift I met Julian in the Chelsea Potter. He asked, 'Where did you get those notes from in the middle of the week?'

'It's my birthday, but don't tell anyone. Let's both have Pimm's.'

'But why don't you want people to know, I would have got you something. What are you doing later?'

'Seeing, you know...'

'What, Phene Man? Does he know it's your birthday?'

'No, I don't want him to.'

'Why not, you're legal, you know, doing it at your age, it's only before you're sixteen he has to worry.'

The landlord came with our Pimm's in half-pint glasses. 'Here we are, hearts, a veritable fruit salad.' As well as ice and mint and cucumber the landlord of the Chelsea Potter always put into Pimm's slices of orange and apple, lemon and cherries. We drank three each.

Julian did not want to go home on his own. 'Do you want to do something else before you go?' he asked hopefully.

'I can't, I need to be somewhere... you know...'

'Yeah, I know, because you're meeting him.'

I did not want Julian to be jealous. Because he was my good friend I wanted him to be happy when I was happy.

'Why don't you go on to the Pheasantry Club?'

'No money. My dad's out tonight and Lalla's God knows where and I haven't got my door key.'

'Here,' I took the change and Ron's note from my bag. 'Here, take this, you can go to the Pheasantry until you know your dad will be home.'

'I can't take that, it's your birthday money.'

'Yes, you can, I don't want it, honestly.'

On the Radnor Walk corner Julian, swaying slightly, said, 'Happy birthday, Suse, you're the best.' He kissed me on the cheek and a car hooted at us and then we turned in opposite directions down the Kings Road.

*

'Have you had a lot to drink, Susie?' Jack asked me.

'No, not much, it was somebody's birthday at work, that's all.'

'When is your birthday, by the way?'

'The first of March.'

'St David's Day, then.'

'Yes, I suppose, when is yours?'

'November the fourteenth. It means that I am a moody soul with a darker side, or so they tell me.'

I was light-headed with the Pimm's. Julian had said that the sugar in the lemonade sent the alcohol into your bloodstream quicker.

'Imagine,' he had said as he tried to spear a maraschino cherry which was eluding his cocktail stick, 'imagine it, the actual bubbles might actually be fizzing in our veins, now. We might feel them popping... pop, pop, poppity pop... Happy birthday, Suse, and many more of them.'

I stood in the middle of the room visualising the coursing of the tawny-coloured bubbles. I felt the sensation of being pleasantly drunk and the anticipation that at any moment Jack would start to touch me. I recalled the events of that morning and of other birthdays and how little I had liked them and, except for the short time with Alison, how little I had liked life in general until I had come to find my father. Apart from the occasions when it was lifted and defaulted by some passage in a book or line in a poem it had always been dreary, as though somehow, through some fault of my own, something lacking in me, I had missed the meaning and the rules that other children found straight away, like the clues in a treasure hunt. Now I seemed to have been saved; I felt that when I looked back it was someone else's life behind me.

I was wearing a T-shirt patterned with stars. It was quite

tight. Jack was easing it over my head. When he undressed me he was very careful always to lift my hair out of the way, so that it did not get pulled by a neckline or snagged on buttons. Sometimes his hands shook.

'So, on St David's Day next you will be all of nineteen years old?'

'Yes.'

'God, but I'm a lucky bastard.'

On Saturday afternoon the Great Gear Trading Company was quiet and I was helping Jimmy to sort out the metal fittings which fixed in the pegboard walls so that traders could hang their goods on display. We sat on the floor in the orange-painted office. The fittings were all tangled and knitted together, thrown carelessly into a cardboard carton.

Jimmy said, 'Bollocks, we'll have to tip the whole lot out to do the job properly.' I began sorting them into piles by size. 'So, when did you lose your virginity then?'

'What?'

'When did you lose it, I've been trying to work it out. When you first came here to ask me for a job I would have put money on your still being a virgin, right? Now, you're very obviously not.'

'How do you know that?'

'Oh come on, Suse, it's just one of those things, you can tell, right, at least a man can. What I've been trying to work out is when, where and with whom?' He spoke the w sounds in an exaggerated, theatrical elocution. 'Which lucky punter in the Potter? They were all sniffing around you, you know.'

'I know. Somebody offered me money to do it with him.'

Jimmy hooted with delight. 'Who, who was it? No, don't tell me, let me guess.'

'Actually, I promised him I wouldn't tell anyone.'

'Fucking hell, Suse, the man was trying to buy your body, I don't think you're under any moral obligation to him.'

'Okay then, it was Gordon.' Gordon was a property developer with a number of large schemes in Fulham. He often sat at the bar of the Chelsea Potter, his long grey hair straggly and at odds with his fashionable, expensive clothes.

Jimmy hooted again. 'I love it, I love this day! Can you believe it, Mr Big, having to pay for it! What did he actually say?'

'He said that I had a beautiful face, and that he would pay for it. He said he'd done that before, you know, paid and stuff, with a loo attendant at the Dorchester, but they got caught and she got the sack. He said he spoke up for her to the management but it made no difference.'

Jimmy was laughing so hard there were tears in his goat-pale eyes. 'You wait till he comes in poncing around in his Piero di Monzi suit next time, you fucking wait mate, *schadenfreude*, do I love it, yes I fucking do.'

'Don't tell him that you know.'

'It's all right, I won't let on. Did he, by the way, with you?'

'No! No, it's not him.'

'So who then, is it somebody in the pub? How can you be so good at secrets at your age?'

'No, it's nobody in the pub.'

'It better not have been some spotty youth that tools around your school gates with his tongue hanging out. You want someone who knows his way around, especially when it's your first. God, Suse, you could have had me, it makes my balls ache to think about it. So, is he good? Do you like it?'

I smiled down at the shining heap of silver fixtures. 'I'm not saying anything.'

'It's all right, you don't need to.'

*

When you are young people upbraid you for the use of superlatives. 'How can you possibly know', they will say, 'How can you make such sweeping statements', and 'You'll learn, one day, you have to compromise in this life'.

People are very stupid; obtuse. After all, you do not qualify your reaction to art or music (unless you are an academic), you respond in the superlative. So it is with love and joy. I knew, with the Easter kiss, that it was the most perfect that I should ever have. In the same way, I knew that on the evening when I lay naked in my father's arms and he read to me from Kenneth Grahame, it was the happiest hour in my life.

'Do you know this book?' he had asked when I picked up from his desk a copy of *Dream Days*. I shook my head, sometimes it is easier to lie if you do it with signs and gestures rather than the spoken word. In my mind there ran a picture of the art nouveau end papers and the boy's thick-nibbed pen: John (Jack) ap Rhys Owen.

'I've always loved it,' he said, 'especially the "Reluctant Dragon" story. I had a copy once, when I was a boy, a smashing edition with these sort of Rackham-esque illustrations. Don't know what became of it. Anyway, I've set myself a project, I'm going to do a set of drawings from it. Just for me probably, though I may approach the author's estate, if they turn out well enough.'

I wished that I could tell him that the first copy was safe. 'Do you miss it?'

'What?'

'The book, the other one.'

'Do I... I don't know, really... No, it's only things I suppose, isn't it, not like people... you can't hang on to everything...'

'Read it to me,' I said, 'read me your favourite story.'

'Really?'

I nodded and so he stretched for the book that lay upon the desk. The cloth binding was a dull orange-brown, and this edition had no illustrations. Jack asked me if I was comfortable. He supported the book with the hand of the arm that was around my shoulders, my head rested upon his chest so that as well as his heartbeat I could feel the sound vibrations as he spoke. He began to read: 'Footprints in the snow have been unfailing provokers of sentiment ever since snow was first a white wonder in this drab-coloured world of ours.'

Sometimes, among schoolchildren at that time, you would hear one charging another with an untruth told: 'You're a born liar,' they would accuse.

I suppose that I was a born liar. I did not want to lie, not to Jack. Sometimes, in the times when I was joined to him, I wanted to tell him the truth. Once he paused and asked me, 'What do you think about, when we're doing this?... In here...' He touched my forehead with his thumb as though there were a smudge there. 'What are you thinking about, in here, Susie?'

Inside my head I might just have been repeating the diminutives of father over and over again.

'You,' I said, 'just you.'

Because I loved him so much and he told me, often, how happy I made him and how lucky, I never saw that what we did was wrong. But I did know that outsiders would fail to understand. In consequence, I knew that I must absolve him from all possible blame by never telling him the truth. I kept Dad and Daddy dumb, unheard inside me.

How many years ago had it been when Christine Threadgold,

thickset and the bully of the junior school, had challenged me at the playground gate. 'Where's your dad?' she demands. Her fringe is ginger and her cardigan salmon pink; already she has the mannerisms of the Battersea mothers, chin up, bottom out.

'Away at sea,' I say; so I was a liar even then. 'He is, he's away at sea.' It was an expression I had heard a post office crony of my mother's use about the husband of some third party whom they disparaged and picked to pieces over the aerograms and parcel labels and scarlet-beaked bottles of Gloy glue.

'I don't believe you,' says Christine and she is echoed by the mothers' meeting chorus of her supporters. Her own father, small with a Useless Eustace grin and hair soap and water slicked back, is sometimes seen following the Threadgold women through the market stalls of Northcote Road.

'He is,' I repeat fervently and look up to the white London sky above the roof lines and chimneys, 'he really is.' And tears try to come pushing out with the force of my conviction.

'My love,' says Jack when his voice is husky and he takes me into his arms, 'my love, my own best girl.'

And, born liar that I am, I became most adept at evading any direct questions from him about my home life or family. I had told him that my mother had died in an accident when I was very small. He was gentle and sympathetic, he said, 'I am so sorry, Susie, it must have been very difficult for you, I'm sure.' And I, looking beyond his thin kind face, recalled her as she threw the dolls' cake and told me that he was dead and a useless bastard and let the sketchbook be ruined; I found it hard to conjure any expression of wistfulness. I told Jack that my surname was James, which was Alison's name. Just as on that first night in the Phene, when I had pictured the Prince of Wales Drive flat for my home, so I pictured Julian's father for the role of mine. Fleetingly and coincidentally, whenever I did so, I gained an understanding of what a good parent Peter was. I said that there was an aunt that stayed sometimes, to look after us. Jack did not ask me very much about them; I guessed that he would have imagined the reaction of my relations to the age difference between us.

When Jack said that I was very bright and should be at university instead of working as a waitress I made reference to some vague problems I had had, over teachers. 'But I will think about it, later on,' I told him. I knew that if he could have found out about Oxford he would make me go. I also knew that I would be quite incapable, physically, of going so far away from him. One day when I was looking for my hairbrush the annotated copy of *Richard II* fell out of my bag.

'Are you reading this, Susie?'

I took it back before he could find my name and form number and date of issue in the front. 'Yes, I did it at school. I liked it so much that sometimes I read it again.'

'You are a funny mixture,' Jack said.

A few days later he was reading the paper and he made an exclamation of pleased triumph.

'Do you know what, there's going to be a new production of *Richard II* by the RSC, real landmark stuff, two actors taking it in turns as Richard and Bolingbroke. I could take you to see it, would you like that?'

'Yes, I would, very much.'

He never did. On the first night, when Richard Pascoe and Ian Richardson bowed to applause on the stage of the Aldwych theatre, my father Jack was already dead.

Although my occupation in those months was ceaseless I never felt any fatigue. I worked and revised and sat my exams; I practised endless complicated deceits and I travelled miles backwards and forwards across the Thames bridges. In my father's bed the passion and desire for him, in my body and in my head, was close to a kind of derangement. On the narrow mattress whole hours would pass when I was detached from the real world and from reason. I might have committed any crime for him. Truly, it was a form of possession. And yet I was never weary, rather, I was quickened and energised by that life I led. Perhaps it was the deep sleeps that I slept beside Jack, so cherished and safeguarded as I was. He played me Ella Fitzgerald, and she sang 'Someone to Watch Over Me'.

Sometimes, if I returned home in the evening, I would find the flat filled by a gathering of Ron's friends. In those days there was a structured hierarchy of London's criminals; I expect that it may be different now. Lin had intimated that because members of her boyfriend's family had served as lieutenants to the Brothers Kray, they enjoyed some standing in the underworld. I knew that Scottie the cat burglar was deemed to be a gentleman thief. I had myself heard him expostulate with righteous indignation over the report of a gang who had run down a policeman during a robbery. But among Ron's associates there were criminals of the pettiest kind. These were minor thieves; they traded stolen goods from market stalls, some made a livelihood through illegalities in the motor trade, some organised poker games in lock-up garages on suburban alleyways where weeds grew up through the concrete.

One night I had returned early from Chelsea to revise for my biology paper; biology and chemistry were the only sciences I liked, I detested maths and physics because I found them incomprehensible. The flat was full and smoky and noisy from Ron's new stereogram. He and his friends were especially fond of Dean Martin and Frank Sinatra and Sammy Davis and also of Ray Charles; 'Busted' was being played. Ron broke off from singing along with it to call out, 'Here's a dolly bird, someone get her a drink.'

I shook my head but he took no notice. I sat down on the floor beside the man I knew to be the quietest member of their group. He was called Tommy Sutton; he was a plumber by day and he lived in a road off the south side of the Common with his elderly mother. He was fair-haired and bearded and noticeably neat and softly spoken amid the rest of the company.

'You look as if you find all this a bit much,' Tommy said.

'It's not that, it's just that I have an exam in the morning, biology O level.'

'Does your mum know?' He nodded towards my mother who sat on the other side of the smoky room; she was watching intently as the short man that they called Diddy Dave demonstrated a balancing trick with drinking glasses and beer mats.

'I don't know, probably not.'

'Look, you try and slide out to your room. I'll see if I can persuade this lot to call it a night.'

'Thomas,' Ron called loudly, 'don't you go chatting up that right little raver over there, you know your mum wouldn't like it.' Then he protruded his lips into a pout and bent one hand over at the wrist in a gesture which was supposed to indicate effeminacy.

'Go on,' said Tommy to me.

I managed to leave the gathering without attracting comment. In my room I put my pillow at the foot of the bed so that I could sleep by the open window and let the fresh night air lift the smoke smell out of my hair. Before I settled I made myself review in my head the component parts of the kidneys, lungs, heart and inner ear. Then, only when I was sure that I could repeat each feature without faltering, I allowed myself to think of Jack. How I had learned that when I was above him, even by the minutest of movements I could affect him. I was fascinated to see myself causing these changes in his man's face, watching for it to tighten and grimace and for him to beseech me, on and on, until he had convulsed out all he had into me and his expression became smoothed again and he smiled for me. I believed then that it was all the power that I should ever need.

Next day, in the long, hushed examination hall, I made a good job of the biology paper. I took far more care with diagrams and drawings now that I had sat for hours on the bed watching Jack at work. I saw him conjure small and meticulous acts of magic as he made a story appear upon the blank white page. His infinite patience and the steady, absorbed breathing intensified the quiet of the room, as did the stillness of the cat, sitting sentinel at his side. I thought that one day he would make a picture of himself at the table with the cat and in that picture he made he would be working upon the picture of himself, at the table with the cat.

On the way to Chelsea the bus stopped at Battersea Garage to change drivers. I looked over the road at the dark prison-yard walls of the Morgan Crucibles factory on the riverside. The widower father of a girl in my class had worked there but in the Christmas term he had died. The girl, Joanne, said that it was because of him being widowed, that he could not bear her mother being gone and so he had just given up, he had died of a broken heart. I found it most affecting; I told my mother but she said that it was impossible. 'Nonsense, there's no such thing as dying of a broken heart.'

In bed that night my father made a remark that was supposed to be flippant and light-hearted but it filled me with such panic and terror that I thought I should lose my mind. It happened because I had perfected ways of touching him with such gentleness that when I began it he could hardly tell that my fingers were there at all. His body would incline to me as though by tropism but I would make him wait and keep my touchings as soft as breath. This prolongation could cause him to cry out in sounds that were quite primeval. If I had heard them anywhere else, merely as a bystander, I think I would probably have been afraid. Then, as he gave in and I had the warm stuff running out between my fingers I would kiss him as if our mouths were glued together. Afterwards he made the remark that so terrified me. He said, 'Sometimes, with you, I think I must have died and gone to Heaven.'

Perhaps I was overwrought from the exams. I sat up in the bed and the terror and alarm that seized me prevented me from breathing properly. My mother had told me that he was dead and for years I had believed it to be so. Then I had got him back. Now that he himself spoke of it, and it was presented to me again, I could see only the colour red, the inside eyelid colour and the ambulance blanket scarlet. And I could hear in my head some alarming discordant sound which was like blood rush mixed with the bells of ambulances. I tried over and over again to catch my breath in but it would not go over the top. Also I must have begged him incessantly, 'Don't say that, please don't say that. He is not dead, he is not dead.' Because I begged him so many times the plea took up the rhythm of a prayer that is repeated in decades but the panic between the lines felt like falling down many flights of stairs. Jack stayed very calm. He held my head tight between his two hands so that he was pressing on the bone of the skull and he tried to make me look at him but I could not, for fear, in case it was only his ghost that spoke to me.

'It's all right, Susie, listen to me, it's all right. It was just a foolish thing I said, that's all. Nothing more, nothing worse than that. Come on now, be still.'

He had switched on the desk lamp and for a long time I sat staring at the same patch of the wall. My hand was still sticky but now the stuff was gone cold. The salt from my tears was stinging my cheeks as if they would chap straight away. In my chest I felt a pain like a stitch after running. 'I can't breathe.'

'Yes, you can, just take it easy.'

'No, I can't, I can't breathe properly.'

'I tell you what, we'll go out and get some fresh air. Come on, I'll help you to dress.'

Down in the street the cat materialised out of the shadows of the basement railings. Jack pushed him gently inside the hall. 'Don't you go waking Eunice now,' he said.

In the night some of the colours of the spectrum were missing from the street scene. Jack held my hand and we walked towards Albert Bridge. Oakley Street was quiet and empty; only one taxi passed us, its hire sign turned off. At the building site where they had demolished the Pier Hotel the watchman's lamps glowed red. The bridge was empty and still, a film of dew on its black road surface. For months it had been closed to all traffic for repairs. We passed the wooden notice board that warned troops to break step. We stopped halfway across. Jack leant with his back against the parapet and enclosed me within his arms, now and then lifting strands of my hair so that the cool river night touched my face. 'So, are you steadier now?'

I nodded and leant forward upon his chest.

'Sometimes, with all the things we do, I forget... how very young you still are... my fault, stupid of me.'

I stood and looked from the bridge, up towards the City and across to darkened Cheyne Walk. Along the deserted embankment ran the impish silhouette of a man; perhaps he was a thief. On the other side the park was locked in by gates, beneath our feet the Thames' unhurried tide. The moon was two-thirds full and there were some stars and an aeroplane crossing. I was comforted that what I could see from within my father's arms was the whole world.

Later, sensing that he must be chilled and weary, I reached up for his face and kissed him. The skin of his cheek and his lips was cold and dry. To warm his hands I took them inside the clothes which he had only recently helped me to fasten. He said to me, 'It will be all right, you know. I won't let anything bad happen, little one, I promise.'

'We could go back to the room now, if you like.'

'Yes, let's do that. And do you know what, I have some very questionable Spanish brandy in the cupboard under the sink. I shall put some in hot milk with brown sugar and I shall insist upon you drinking it all up. You will sleep like a top, best beloved.'

$\bigcirc$n the evening of the day that I sat my last O level I found my father very drunk. Someone had left the street door open to the warm air. Haddock the cat lolled over the step and batted his tail warningly as I stepped carefully across him.

In the room Jack was semi prone in the armchair. 'Oh hallo, sweetness, I was going to put on some music but I couldn't find the bloody thing,,,'

One hand hung over the chair arm, wearing a record sleeve like a huge glove. I went to sit on the bed, waiting to see what would happen next.

'God,' he said, 'God, I so badly want to come over there and jump on you but I don't think my dick would work.'

I observed that his hair was dishevelled, sticking out in tufts at the back of his head. Also, intoxication seemed to have softened the lines of his gaunt face; this was oddly in accord with his next remark: 'Drink is a great thing. Drink is a great thing because it blurs the sharp edges...'

He closed his eyes briefly and his face looked quite young and defenceless, as his parents must once have seen it. I inspected my bare legs to see how much the sun had caught them. I had tried to acquire a tan in the Clapham County garden while revising for my exam. It had been Greek Literature in Translation,

Herodotus and *The Odyssey*. I turned my calves. Jack opened his eyes.

'Do you know why I'm so pissed, actually?'

'Because you've had a lot to drink.'

'Hah! Miss Answer-me-back, clever... but no, no actually, it's because I saw my wife today. Before, or after she went to Bentall's which is, as we all know, Kingston's most finest department store...'

Beside him on the painting desk was an opened bottle of red wine; the label read Sans Chi Chi. He poured some into a glass already half full.

'Mind your sketches,' I warned him.

'No, no, you're all right, we're all right, there, that's it.'

He drank some then held it out towards me, 'Share this one, sweetness, don't mind, do you... I can't find another glass. What's yours is mine, mine is yours, all yours, for ever and ever...'

There was a thrill through me at this phrase, albeit it was so slurred.

'She said something that made me think, made me drink.' He laughed miserably at the word play.

'What?'

'It was the do... end of term staff party thing, we're all there, standing round bitching and sniping and passing this filthy stuff... sans souci... sans chi chi... I don't bloody know. Then the Pat Pell woman starts on about someone's doing this with somebody... who's having affairs with who else's spouse... then they all chip in... this that... at it like knives. Then Olive, my wife, do you know what she says...?'

'No, what?'

'She says, oh well, Jack and I, we don't worry about that sort of thing any more, do we, Jack. We've done with all that between the sheets lark... ha ha bloody ha. Rather read a good book nowadays. Too old, she says, past it... she says that I am past it... no one's going to want me, she says...' He looked towards me to focus on my reaction but one of his eyes was semi-closed. 'Christ, I think I'll start smoking again.'

'No, don't do that.'

'Don't you want me to?'

'No.'

'All right then, I won't. But it's a fact, according to bloody Olive, no woman could ever possibly find me attractive any more... ever again. And yet here, here I am, in this room, old and worn out as I may be, and, but I'm with you... you, you who are the most beautiful girl in the world bar none and I am king of the world, king of the bloody world when I bury myself inside you... but you... you won't want me... won't want me, not at all, not on your bloody life...' There was the flicker of an expression across his face which might have prefaced tears or laughing of the uneasy, self-contempt kind.

I decided it was the time to do the thing that Julian and I had discussed weeks before. I thought that if I really found it distasteful I could, until it was over, think about the essay I had written in that morning's exam.

I got up and went across to Jack's chair. I took the wine glass from him and set it out of harm's way. Then I dropped to my knees in front of him.

'What...' he began.

'It's okay,' I said, I watched my fingers at their task. I drew down the heavy brass zip on his cord trousers. I felt for the opening in his underwear. I hesitated for a moment and thought of how that morning I had written that for all the terrible things he does, Homer still manages to make us feel pity for Polyphemus. Then I bowed my head and hid my face and my father wound strands of my hair around his hands like ropes.

When it was over he said, 'Let us lie down together. I want you beside me. I want to hold you.'

I helped him across the little stretch of lino to the bed; his legs were still unsteady. I was holding his arm as if he were old and infirm and I was guiding him across a hospital ward. We lay side by side on the narrow bed and the sounds of people out in the summer evening floated up through the open window. Jack said that I was a miracle and that he had never done anything to deserve me. He dozed and I watched him with such love that through my skin I absorbed the presence of him – his smell and the sound of his breathing and his warmth and the air that he breathed out – like green wood does. Later on he opened his eyes and said, 'Come away with me. Let's go away, you and I, let's run away and live in France.'

'All right.'

'You would too, wouldn't you, just like that.'

'Yes.'

'My dear, sweet girl, it's all so very simple to you, isn't it?'

'Yes,' I said a second time, for it was. Even now, at the distance of all those years, it appears just so. All absolutes are simple.

On an evening in August I knew that I was going to be ill again. Jack had gone away early.

'There's a gallery thing, part of the festival. I have an exhibition so I have to talk to people and be nice. I can't get out of it... you know I would if I could. I'll leave as soon as I decently can...'

The Chelsea Potter had tables out on the pavement in Radnor Walk. The ground was stained with the stickiness of spilt drinks. Julian was anticipating without enthusiasm the water sports holiday for which he would depart next morning. He now had a girlfriend in Putney; they had had sex on the night that they met. Although only a fortnight had passed, Julian was already blasé, or at least he pretended to be so. He had met Jill, the Putney girl, on a bus returning from Knightsbridge. Having finally summoned courage to approach the Estée Lauder counter in Harvey Nichols, he was told that the object of his desire no longer worked there. She had successfully applied for the coveted company post in Nassau.

'It was a real downer, but then I just got on this bus and met Jill.'

I wanted to make him talk and laugh and be amusing to take my mind off the horrible feeling beginning in my throat. The same feverishness that hurried on the infection also hastened my anxieties, which tripped and stumbled one over another. If I became ill with tonsillitis I would have to stay at home, in bed. I would not be able to see my father. I would not be able to tell him why or to telephone from the flat. He would think I had gone and was not coming back or he might seek me out among the quiet lobbies of Prince of Wales Drive. If he did think that I had gone he would believe that I had left him for good, as he had once told me that I would. He would think that the time had come for me to take up that permission that he had tried so carefully and so fairly to offer me when we began. He would believe what Olive had told him about no longer being desirable; he would be convinced that she must be right because once he had relied upon her so much and I would not be there to show him otherwise and prove her wrong. He would start drinking again and he would not be able to work. I must not let it happen. I tried to sound very bright, with Julian. 'So, what is it like then, is it how you thought it would be?'

'Yeah, it was really quick, at first, but not as bad as it might have been. Jill has done it before, so she knows stuff.'

'Do you want another drink?' I determined to see if I could block the pain away with neat vodka and ice.

'Okay, just a quick one. I haven't packed yet and my dad will start getting twitchy.' Inside there were few people. Seated at the bar the drummer was playing at spoof with Barry the painter. On the stretcher of his stool his feet were bare and very dirty. 'So, are you still seeing Mr Phene?'

'Yes.'

'Isn't he, I don't know, much older, don't you want to go with other people sometimes? Like boys of our age for instance.'

'No. I don't want anyone else. I'm going to stay with him, always.'

'Yeah, well, you say that now.'

'I mean it. I will never, ever leave him.'

My emphasis must have been fierce, Julian looked taken aback. 'Okay, okay, I was only saying, but anyway, isn't he married?'

'Yes, but that doesn't matter, she doesn't live in London.'

We took our drinks back to a pavement table and sat for a while longer in desultory silence. Julian picked at the sole of his shoe. On the opposite pavement a couple started to have an argument. The man's hips were very narrow and his permed hair curled halfway down his back.

'You're just a slag, Vanessa, d'you know that.' He was leaning forward from his sapling waist to berate her.

The girl was holding on to the pole of the Belisha beacon; they were both kohl-eyed and seemed to be drugged. On other occasions Julian and I would have enjoyed watching such a scene, even making a wager on which protagonist would come off best. We had still that unfeeling adolescent myopia which generally allowed us to see only the pantomime amusement of such incidents, without any comprehension of the ramifications of people's misfortunes or discomforts. That evening, however, the public row seemed only discordant and uncomfortable. Soon afterwards Julian and I parted on the corner of Flood Street. I knew that we had each found the other to be dull and a disappointment. If I had not been so preoccupied by the fear of being ill this failure in our companionship would have made me sadder and sorrier than it did; I would have felt the burden of responsibility for putting it right.

Next morning I was waiting on the doctor's doorstep for his wife to unlock the door. He gave me penicillin and he looked me up and down as though to indicate that he could say more. I must have been a strange and dishevelled sight. I wore the clothes of the day before because I had felt too ill to undress. I had not removed my make-up and probably I smelled of stale sex. With enormous difficulty I swallowed two of the penicillin tablets as I walked through the sunny morning streets. The milk float was finishing its round and a woman cleaning windows called out some cheerful comment to its driver. I was glad to find that the flat was empty. I told myself that if I lay down and concentrated single-mindedly I could force the infection to go away. My throat had swollen too tight to swallow.

'You're disgusting,' Lin had said when I had to let saliva drool onto the pillow. I did not want that to happen in Jack's bed.

I woke up to noises from the kitchen and my mother looked in at me. 'Oh, you're in, are you? What are you doing in bed at this time of day?'

'I've got the tonsil thing again. I'll be fine though, I've got some stuff from the doctor.'

Two tears came from the pain of the effort of speaking the sentences. She said, 'If it's not one bloody thing it's another. Do you want tea?'

I could only shake my head. I heard her go back into the

kitchen, banging the kettle on the gas ring, not especially in anger, but because she always performed tasks like that with force.

At some time during the night I woke again. People in a neighbouring house were having a party and it had spilled out into the back garden. I looked down at the light falling on women in long flowered dresses. A curly-haired man was passing among them with glasses and the music of a classical guitar was playing beneath the chatter. I got up for water to take more penicillin. I did not know whether the sour taste was my own mouth or the London tap water which had been lying, warmish, in the old lead pipes. I tested how I felt, reviewing my body part by part. I thought that the tonsillitis infection was abating but I sensed that there was something else wrong. The penicillin was supposed to be two to start and then one four times per day but I calculated that I must have missed some doses by sleeping through and so I took two more tablets.

When I woke again I could smell that my mother was cooking a Sunday roast. The air was full of the odour of lard which she heated to smoking point to roast the potatoes. I felt very strange. When I lifted my head from the pillow there seemed to be another head inside it, moving separately from the outer case.

I told myself that a bath would help. I undressed and as I did so I gasped to see that my body was covered with livid scarlet blotches. The shape and distribution was like the patterning on a giraffe's skin or dappled sunlight beneath a summer tree. Instinctively I pulled a towel around me to hide it although there was no one there to see. I knew that there must be something seriously wrong. Momentarily I was afraid enough to consider calling out and seeking the help of my mother or Lin. Then, holding on to the cold rim of the bath, I realised that if I admitted that there was a problem while I was in the flat it could preclude any contact with my father. I was appalled to think how close I had been to giving in to fear and thus to separation from him. I despised myself for such weakness. Slowly and deliberately I washed and dressed. My hands shook so much that I had to support my elbow with the other arm in order to apply make-up.

In the living room there was the malty smell from beer bottles and chatter on the radio. It almost seemed then that it could be a comfortable and homely world and for a moment I wished that I was not an outsider.

'Are you in for dinner? Here, beat this.' My mother put a basin of yellow Yorkshire pudding batter and a spoon in my hands. I leant against a chair back for support.

'No, thank you. I'll see if they need me at work, then I might go down to Allison's.'

The big tablespoon was stamped with the name Hotel Somerset. During the war my grandmother had bought goods from the sales held to dispose of the equipment from bombed-out hotels.

'Quicker than that, for God's sake, don't slop it. Oh, give it here.'

'Bye then.' Again I wavered, tempted to seek help. I feared that I might fall over in the street.

'Yes, off you go then... it's all bloody lumpy now...'

I turned away and left my mother frowning as she began to fiercely beat at her batter. Out in the sunlight white bubble and bar shapes floated over my vision. I decided that I would cross the Common for the bus, to be seen by fewer people. I walked over the hummocky stretch of grass where groves of hawthorn grew. On one slope a teenage couple were lying wrapped together. My balance was disturbed and I veered far too close to where they lay; they looked up in annoyance as I passed and their eyes were like currants in faces of dough. At the centre of the Common the bandstand rose as for a shipwrecked swimmer, with the distance between never diminishing. At last I reached Cedars Road and I leant against the concrete bus stop for support, pretending to be lounging in Sunday idleness. When the bus came I sensed the conductress staring at me and I was afraid that she would make me get off. I sat looking resolutely forward on the top deck, fixing on the brick chimneys of the power station. When the bus stopped on the bridge I looked down and noticed a patch of flotsam in the water, bits of wood and plastic and gull feathers; the current, in chevrons, worried at the edges.

From Sloane Square I walked behind Kings Road, seeking out the privacy of the small rich streets that I had learned so well in the spring. I wished that Julian was not away and that I could find him in the Chelsea Potter to help me. I knew that despite us being out of sorts last night he would seem young and flippant and that he could stop me feeling as if I was slipping away, like the mucky white feathers on the flotsam island.

When I reached Jack's doorstep in Oakley Street I cried with relief; although there was no sensation in my face to feel the course of the tears as they fell, I saw them dropping and splashing on the stone. All afternoon I sat there. Someone had not picked up their newspaper and whenever a passerby looked at me curiously I pretended to be reading it; I could see nothing but a grey mass, the colour of egg boxes. Once or twice I folded back the hem of my jeans to see that the red markings on my legs were more intense. I did not dare to look at my face in the mirror from my bag. I had parted my hair at the neck of my blouse and pulled it forward to hide as much as I could.

I may have slept or I may not have been fully conscious. Suddenly I saw that Jack's car was there where it had not been before. At first he did not notice me. He leant in to take a VG carrier bag from the back seat. It was filled with windfall apples.

When he found me on the step he raised me up by the elbows. 'My dear child, what have you done?'

I was more frightened by his reaction than anything that had gone before. 'I'm not sure, but it's okay, I think. Really, it's okay.'

'I don't think it is, Susie.' Until that moment I had not realised that he might insist upon me going home. 'Let's get you inside.'

He made me sit down on the bed; the room, closed up all weekend, smelled of sun-warmed air and fabrics. 'Stay there, I'm going to ask Eunice to take a look at you. She nursed during the war.'

I knew that more tears of relief were issuing from my eyes but the nerve endings in my face were still not working. I wiped it with handfuls of my hair.

Jack was saying, 'She's here... if you wouldn't mind just taking a look... I'm not sure what can be wrong...'

I was conscious of disliking myself again, this time because I was causing my father to look lost and old and grey and anxious. Towards Eunice I felt gratitude because she was brisk and business-like and her face gave nothing away. 'Are you allergic to anything?'

'I don't know.'

'When did this start, can you remember?' From her tone of voice and the way she sought my concentration I knew that she thought I was losing consciousness. I did feel that I was sliding away but it was no longer frightening, in Jack's room; now the sensation seemed amusing. I remembered the 1962 and 1963 winter of heavy snow when I would deliberately throw myself down on the white heaped drifts because I knew that it would not hurt me.

'Try and remember, Susie.' She had hold of one of my hands

and she was tapping on it quite rhythmically. She reminded me either of the maths teacher or the music teacher, I knew that both of them thought I was a dunce, and again I wanted to laugh; the feeling of sliding backwards was really very funny.

Then Jack leant down by my shoulder and spoke close to my ear. 'Listen, Susie, you must try to remember, try to remember and then you can tell me, can't you, you can tell Jack. Come on Susie, try, for me, won't you, please try, Susie.'

I was used to doing what he coaxed me to do. 'After I started the pills. I was getting better.'

Eunice again, 'What pills was it, Susie, were they penicillin?'

'Yes, that's what I always have.'

'Jack, I think St George's might be a good idea.' I saw the way she looked at him.

'Could you... would you mind?'

'Of course I will.'

I was glad to see that she was being so kind to my father.

It was the only time that I ever travelled in the old Citroën. St George's Hospital was in the process of its long remove from Hyde Park Corner to Tooting Bec. In the Casualty department a number of the bays had already been stripped, you could see where curtain rails and lockers had been dismantled. So that I would not forget and give something away I tried to keep my concentration by determining whether it was every alternate bay that had been removed but the white geometry continued to dance in my eyes and sometimes my sight shut down altogether. There were pins and needles in my hands and, periodically, up and down my arms, as though the sensation was thrown over me in bucketfuls. I felt as if my fingers were made of lint rolls so that no matter how tightly I bent them there was no sensation of holding on to anything. I must have gripped Jack's arm very hard when we walked from the car because days later bruises remained, yet he seemed as insubstantial as air and shadow.

I kept catching at the thought that I must weight down certain lies in my head for when they asked me questions; when I had revised in the Clapham County garden on breezy days I had anchored the pages of my notes with stones and bits of stick. An immature woodlouse had scurried out on to Salisbury's speech: '...with the eyes of heavy mind, I see thy glory like a shooting star...' Facts needed to be altered, where I was born, where I lived, my family name. I must remember. 'Fall to the base earth from the firmament. Thy sun sets weeping in the lowly west...' The brickwork of the corridor walls was painted grey-green. With the colour and the pipes and the dials it was reminiscent of a film set for the inside of a submarine.

A blue nurse said, 'Bring her through, Mother,' and for a moment none of us understood what she meant.

Then Jack half rose from one of the canvas and metal chairs and spoke to Eunice. 'Is that all right... will you go in with her?'

'It's probably simpler if I do.'

The nurse handed her a clipboard with a form to fill in my details. I tried hard to fix upon Eunice's face but she did not look at me. She showed no hesitation over completing the task. 'She's been taking penicillin, Nurse.'

As the nurse leant to take my pulse Eunice edged the clipboard within my wavering vision. She had given me the Oakley Street address and the day of my birth as the first of March. Jack must have told her that, he was so pleased and inordinately proud about it being, as he believed, St David's Day. The year tallied with my being eighteen. And for that one night only I was, after all, Susanna Rhys Owen. I began to slide again.

A tousled registrar had appeared. 'Well you're a sight for sore eyes, young lady, aren't you? You did right to bring her in, Mother. Severe allergic reaction to penicillin.' He lifted the clothing from my back and I sensed the heat rising from the blotches. As he stuck an injection in above my hip he turned to Eunice and said, 'Nick of time, to be frank. We'd keep her in but we're rather stretched. So long as there'll be someone with her all the time to keep an eye on things. It should settle down now but any worries, just bring her straight back.'

Out in the corridor Jack stood up and looked old. Eunice nodded to reassure him.

'Right, I'll go and bring the car round then.'

When he had gone I said, 'I need to make a phone call.'

'Don't worry about it now, we can do it later.'

'No, I have to make it when Jack's not here.'

She looked at me and formed her face as if to speak but then did not. She supported me to the telephone on the wall and found me a sixpence. She held my arm while I dialled but turned her face away to indicate that she was not trying to listen. I thanked God that it was Ron who answered because he was too stupid to ask for details, and anyway, he did not care enough to question anything that I told him.

'I'm going to stay at my friend's, at Alison's, for a few days, can you tell...'

'Righty ho. Do you want to speak to your mum at all?'

'No, that's okay, if you could just say...' I put the receiver down and swayed back on Eunice with relief.

'Is that it, have you done all that you need to do?'

Jack returned. 'Listen, Susie, I never thought to ask... would you rather we just took you home?'

'No, we can't do that,' said Eunice, 'they're all away, Susie was just telling me, weren't you, Susie?'

On the way back to Chelsea the car seemed to be moving through a tank of water or across the bottom of the sea. When I thought that it was travelling down Kings Road I very much wanted to see the familiar yellow lit bar through the big window of the Chelsea Potter but I was unable to move my head at the right time.

Back in the room Jack put me to bed. He changed my clothes for the shirt of grey stripes which he often wore. It must have been washed and ironed in Suffolk. It smelled of drying out of doors. Eunice came in wearing a man's dressing gown of brown plaid; she carried a pillow and blanket for Jack's chair. I heard her say, 'Doesn't matter what time it is, Jack, anything you need.' At the door she turned to me. 'Sleep well, Susie, you're going to be all right now.'

Jack sat up in the chair all night long. I saw the outline of him in the dark each time I woke. I did feel very ill but nothing frightened me with my father being there, a hand's reach away. I tested out the thoughts that I used to have about dying when I was ill and I found that there was no fear there any more. From time to time I heard him move in the chair, trying to shift his long body into a more comfortable position. When I felt sleep taking me over it was like deliberately falling in the snow again.

Somewhere near dawn I must have gone into a deeper sleep. When I woke again it was day and on the landing the telephone was ringing. As he passed the bed Jack touched the cover with his hand and gently said, 'It's all right, little one, go back to sleep now.'

He answered the telephone, stretching the wire so that he could stand just on the threshold of the room with it. I knew it was going to be Olive. I listened to him talking to her in that matter-of-fact way that people have when they are used to communicating with each other and dealing with everyday life together. They expect nothing unexpected. I knew that from time to time he would look over at the bed and so I kept my eyes closed and pretended to be asleep again.

'No, no, I won't be able to do that, I have a job that I must finish. It's the Housman thing, I told you about it, that's on top of the lecture notes for Saturday, I haven't finished those yet.'

Her voice was merely a signal of sound, I could not distinguish words, but the tone was deeper and also livelier than I had expected it to be.

'Yes, I appreciate that, it would be pleasant to go together, but it simply can't be done, I'm too busy.'

There was her sound again and he just repeated a 'Yuh, yes, I know' response once or twice, and abstractedly worried at a patch of paintwork on the doorframe with the side of his thumbnail; then, 'What about Mr Mitchell, has he been to look at the boiler yet?'

She must have retorted quite snappily.

'Look, Liv, I know you're put out and cross, I know you're disappointed, and I'm sorry for that, truly I am, but what I've got on has to take precedence...'

I listened to the tone of this woman's disappointment down the line from Suffolk, irritable and discarded, somewhere in her rural morning. I smiled; and then, in her husband's bed, I curled and stretched and curled again like a cat before I slipped back into sleep.

Jack had pink roses sent.

'The house where I grew up, in Treorchy, which is a town in Wales, was called Rosemount, and for years I thought it must be because there were always roses. Everywhere you looked, there were bowls and vases of roses. My mother loved them. It smelt wonderful. As you came into the dining room, the French windows were always slightly ajar and there were long white muslin curtains that lifted in the breeze. There was always a coal fire in the grate, no matter what time of year, and there, in the middle of this big long polished table, would be a mass of roses, a great bowlful of them, in the centre.' I watched him, seeing into the room in his memory. 'Anyway, I thought if anyone should have roses today it was you, so here we are.'

The roses were fat sugar-pink confectionery coloured buds on long dark stems. I wish that I had pressed one to keep.

'The scent will come, when they open a bit.'

He put them on the bedside table.

'I have never had flowers before, thank you.'

I knew why his mother must have moved through the house, placing the roses; it was in order to remember her dead child. Ora's middle name was Rose.

In the morning Jack was wearing the navy blue jersey without a shirt underneath. It made his neck look older, the skin seemed coarser and redder. 'I'll need to go out today, there are things you should have, and I need another shirt. Eunice says she will take a few hours off this morning, she'll come and keep you company. I don't want you left alone.'

Haddock insinuated himself through Jack's legs in the half-open doorway. 'Not you, you bastard, you're unhygienic.' Jack made to grab him but the cat rippled away from his grasp.

'Can he stay, actually?'

I thought that it might be awkward, alone with Eunice, and that Haddock would prove a diversion. The cat sprang onto the pillow behind me. Eunice came in but Jack seemed reluctant to leave. He said, 'Susie seems much better this morning, but I'll hurry back.'

'We'll be fine, Jack, take your time,' Eunice assured him. Being alone with her did not seem awkward; she had brought a pack of cards.

'Do you play rummy? No? Well, I'll show you.'

Jack appeared again. 'Forgot my car keys.' He stood looking undecided while Eunice dealt cards expertly onto one of his painting boards which she had set on the bedcover.

'Are you sure you'll be all right then?' he asked.

'Of course we'll be all right, Jack. Bugger off, do, and get your groceries.'

For a time we spoke only about the game. Concisely, she explained the rules to me. 'For the first game, I'll explain to you as we go along, and help you score. After that, you're on your own, kid.'

She was a determined opponent and therefore it was the more pleasurable when I did win a hand.

'Your deal, Susie. Did you get it all squared, with your telephone call?'

'Yes, I did.'

'I've known Jack for years, he's the best.'

'I know he is.'

'He is a good friend of mine, a dear friend.' She did not look up from the seven cards in her hand as she spoke.

I had never had the chance to be so honest with an adult before. I said, 'You are testing me, aren't you?'

'Yes, Susie, I am. You are not always truthful, are you?'

'No, I'm not, because I can't be. But you must believe that I'm never going to leave him, not ever. I can't bear being away from him.'

She did look up then. 'That's all right, there's no need to upset yourself. I did think that you were serious. I just wanted to make sure, for Jack's sake. Come on, off you go, deal.'

Jack returned with carrier bags. He was so relieved to find us as he had left us that he affected to be semi-seriously indignant and curmudgeonly. 'I've just bought a shirt from that benighted Jean Machine place you go to, Susie. It's absolute daylight robbery, for God's sake, outrageous... they're only secondhand clothes when all's said and done. Stone the bloody crows...'

He had gone in behind the kitchen curtain to change into the purchased shirt of washed-out denim, muttering still. Eunice snorted and we both began to laugh; he emerged from behind the curtain, buttoning the cuffs. 'It's a very nice shirt, Jack,' she said.

'Bloody well ought to be, at that price.'

He had bought orange juice in a big glass jar which he insisted that I drink. Then he came and sat on the end of the bed and joined in the card game with us. He had to lounge his long body at an angle and Haddock stalked across the played-out cards to climb and lie upon his hip, kneading it with his claws so that Jack swore. We sat all together for the rest of the morning. Eunice was exceptionally skilled at a number of card tricks and sleight of hand. I felt regret when it came time for her to leave for Peter Jones. Jack was busy in the kitchen when she leant over the bed to tidy away the cards.

I said, 'Thank you, for everything – you know...'

'Don't mention it. And if ever there's anything you want to talk about, you know where I am, Susie. Jack, I'm off now, you mind you don't spill anything on your nice shirt.'

Jack said that I must eat, and he made me lunch, which was sections of different fruits and foods cut small and arranged in segments on a large white plate. One of the sections was logan-berries; two leaves had been left on in the punnet so he had placed them, soft and grey-green, on the rim of the plate beside the piled berries.

We listened to the William Hardcastle news programme on the radio. When it was over he set out the notes and slides for the lecture he was to give for the festival in Suffolk but he did not begin any work. He kept the chair turned towards the bed and sat watching me. 'You know, I can't help staring at you, when you have no make-up on... I mean, I look at you a lot as it is, but when...' He made the movement of a downward stroke across his face, a mime artist's gesture. 'It's absolutely fascinating, I can see things there that usually you try to hide...'

I began to feel uneasy, anxious at what it was that he might be able to see in my face. I feared lest it could be a resemblance to my mother; she would never have worn make-up, except for Pond's face powder and an occasional gash of lipstick, its consistency congealed. Eye make-up she considered was for tarts. Or perhaps, I thought, he might see traces of Ora, the dead sister, her likeness taken by the portrait photographer, summoned hurriedly from Pontypridd, so that her stricken mother could look upon the likeness and try to pretend that her child was only sleeping. I felt it imperative to divert him. 'Can you come to bed now?'

'No, no I can't, you're not well enough for that sort of thing.'

'I think I am. The blotches have pretty much gone.' I knelt up on the bed and unbuttoned the grey-striped shirt and let it fall back from my shoulders. 'Look, see, they've almost disappeared,' I said, twisting so that I might survey my back.

'No, Susie, this really doesn't seem right.' He had come to lean over the bed and was gently reinstating the shirt around my shoulders.

'Why doesn't it seem right to you, Jack?'

'Because... because, one, you were half-dead yesterday, two, because it's broad daylight out there and I have these benighted lecture notes to finish and three... three is because you only look about twelve without that stuff on your face.'

'Okay.' Meekly, I lay back upon the pillows. Jack stood beside the bed, tall and undecided like an awkward visitor. I sighed and stretched under the snuff-brown cover which lay spread out like a relief map.

'I suppose I could just lie down with you for a little while, that wouldn't hurt. A sort of siesta if you will...'

'Okay,' I said again. The end of the fever had made me thirsty. I watched him undress. He was close enough for me to lift a hand without effort and touch him, as you would a window pane, when you are idly following the course of raindrops down the glass.

Sometimes, on the occasions without urgency, I used to look at his body and consider the thought that I had come from there, that Jack had made me. Brought forth in iniquity. But there was, to me, no deviancy in my returning, again and again, to this place where I had begun. Indeed, in my mind it was a Manichaean opposition to wrongdoing, because what I did, I did out of love. And it was a love which was all but unbearable, I couldn't help it if I tried. And it was instinct too, I suppose. People would say different, but I know that there was nothing else I could have done. I believe that for a time I was blessed because the person that loved me so was the person always so loved by me; nothing else. In the Editor's Notes to the school's old brown-edged Penguin editions of Greek literature there was a section on logic and an explanation of syllogisms. I tried to turn Jack into one.

I loved the man that I knew was the best man in the world.

That man loved me.

Therefore, I must be lovable.

Jack made me viable in two senses.

I pushed his lips open with my tongue. My father said to me, 'Your mouth tastes of berries, it seems apt, somehow.'

The following day he said, 'You're well enough for some fresh air this morning, I think. Shall we go across to the park?'

First he washed my hair for me. There was no shower in the

bathroom, he made me sit on the cork-topped stool by the basin and lean my head back. He had rolled up the sleeves of the Jean Machine shirt. 'We must be quick, we don't want you to get a chill.'

But once he had started he became transfixed by the way my hair floated in the water, playing with the strands like seaweed and curling them around his fingers. He was rapt in his attention. My neck ached from leaning back but I would not have said so.

Afterwards I sat by the window while he dried my hair on a rough white towel. 'There's so much of it, it will take for ever. Shall I brush it for you?'

At the Ricci Burns salon on Kings Road they told you never to brush your hair when it was wet because it stretched it and gave you split ends, but I did not want him to stop so I said nothing. I heard how his breathing changed and I watched him looking at me. He was so entranced.

I recalled what my mother had said, about the other women, especially the one in Pont Street with the silver swizzle stick.

'Did you have a lot of girlfriends, when you were young?'

He smiled, 'Yes... yes, I suppose I did really. More than my fair share, anyway.'

'Was there ever one special one?'

'No, no there wasn't. For that I had to wait until I was old, didn't I.'

In Battersea Park we walked along the path beside the river. To our right the yellow painted concrete areas left over from the Festival of Britain looked now as redundant and disregarded as the derelict emplacements on beaches, erected for the defence of the south coast.

We stopped to lean on the wall and look down on the water. The floating restaurant boat, the *Sloop John B*, was moored below us. On board someone was moving crockery and a radio played

'American Pie'. My father said that he liked the song. 'One verse is supposed to be about Kennedy, so they say.'

When the song had finished we walked on along the path. I had my arm through his and I held his upper arm as well, with my other hand. We had not often walked outdoors together; we learned to match the other's pace, our footsteps in rhyme. Every so often I inclined my thigh sidewards so that it was against him in his stride. In the London air there was that sense of noise and populace that it always has on days that promise heat, when the doors and windows of buildings and cars are opened and people lie on patches of grass with radios playing. From across the park someone had started to call my name; for a moment, because being ill and being in the room in Oakley Street had been another world, I did not recognise the voice, nor did I realise that it was me being called. Then briefly I was alarmed but I saw that it was Julian, walking his mother's Dalmatian dog. Jack gently extricated his arm and retreated apart from us, appearing to be absorbed in the river view. Julian was delighted to see me.

'So, Susie, you and Mr Phene man, what are you up to?'

'Oh, you know... anyway, I thought you were away still.'

'I was supposed to be, but my dad did something to his back on a dive so we had to come home early. Are you coming to the Potter tonight?'

'I might, I'm not sure, I was ill and stuff.' Even though I would enjoy Julian's company, I did not intend to go. I wanted to be closed in the room in Oakley Street again.

'So, are you two still together and everything?'

We each and separately looked across at Jack. I knew how differently we were seeing him; I supposed that Julian primarily noticed his age in the bright glare of the sunlight.

'Yes, we are. He's been taking care of me while I've been ill. How's Jill?'

'I'm going to see her this afternoon. She has the place to herself when her parents are out at work.'

'I'm pleased for you that it's all worked out so well.'

We parted and I watched him walk away across the grass, whistling and calling to the dog running in the distance. Suddenly he stopped and turned back. 'Hey, Susie, how did your exams go?'

'Okay,' I nodded, willing him to go away again.

'Good, mine too,' he beamed.

I counted the paces along the path until Jack would ask, 'What exams, Susie?'

'Nothing.'

'I thought you had left school some time ago.'

'I have, ages and ages ago. These were just re-sits. I didn't say anything in case they went badly, that's all.'

'But they didn't go badly, they went well?'

'Okay, I think.'

'Good, that's good for you. I wish you'd tell me things, Susie.'

Jack had piled the windfall apples in a pottery bowl on the painting desk. Some of the unripened skins were bumpy, greenish brown and frog-like.

'The sun through the window glass will sweeten them up a bit. This variety is Lord Lambourne, I think.' Using the penknife from his pocket he cut one of them into quarters for me while he scanned the newspaper. 'It is the universities section today. Have you decided what you are going to do?'

'No, not really.'

I thought of the envelope that had arrived and all my exam marks being A, except maths and physics, which had been deemed U for unclassified.

'But you must think about it. What do your family say?'

'Nothing, we don't really talk.'

'You have to take opportunities.'

Oxford was too far away from Jack.

'I wouldn't want to go away, not from here, not from you.'

'But, Susie, this isn't just a matter of here and now, it's your future.'

'I couldn't, I don't want to leave you... this room...'

'This room will always be here.'

I shook my head.

'Susie, the world isn't going to stop turning because we don't spend every single day together.'

I shook my head again.

'Life won't end for you, I promise.'

He was wrong.

'Susie...'

He thought that if he said any more, I would start to cry.

'Can you cut me up another apple, please?'

As the beginning of the school year approached I decided that I would not go back at all. Returning home for clothes one day I saw that a letter had arrived from Oxford. The mark for my scholarship paper had been excellent, it said; I was therefore awarded a place to study for the degree of Literae Humaniores. We were invited to attend an open day at the appointed college. Included was a map with travel directions for road or rail and a detailed timetable for the day, the people we would meet, the library we would visit and where we would have lunch. Although I had no intention of going, I imagined what a party we should make if we did; presumably my mother would insist on Ron driving us in the learner car or the van he used for his night security work. She would be short-tempered and resentful and people would think that Ron was my father. I would feel hot with shame and appear dumb and doltish in my embarrassment. I thought that I was glad that it would not happen.

The manageresses at The American Dream asked me to work more shifts. Mireille had returned to France to commence a degree in History and Politics. I hardly went home at all. The days with Jack took on a pattern. The one single room in Oakley Street became an abridged version of domestic life.

Sometimes in the early morning before the traffic started my father took me for walks along the embankment. We stopped to watch the river mist rising and he showed me where, a century before, Whistler must have stood to plan the Battersea paintings. Also he told me that when his drinking had been very bad he had often found himself walking by the river in the early mornings, without memory of the night before. 'But that was a long, long time ago,' he said.

On the way back from the walks we went to the old-fashioned baker's on the corner of Bywater Street to buy breakfast. There were grilles in the pavement and the bread smell rose from the basement ovens on gusts of warmth. I thought that this was how my life would be for ever; it was exactly as I had always wished it to be.

Sometimes, before Jack began work at the desk and I went to open the restaurant, we went back to bed. I could lie for ages on the cover, just kissing him, taking myself into some sort of trance, away from ordinary time. The rest of my body would ache in its suspended animation, like being made to stand still as a child while the hem of a dress is pinned, but all my concentration was focused in the intricate work of my mouth and the small, hidden darts of my tongue which might find sweet crumbs from the breakfast we had taken. At other times we gave each other little episodes and envelopes of pleasure wherever we happened to be. I know that Eunice saw us on the stairs one day and that she stepped back inside her room until we were done. I hoped that we did not make her late for work.

In the room the fireplace had been covered over with a sheet of plywood, but Jack said that he would speak to the landlord so that we could open it up again and when the weather was properly cold we could have real fires in the grate.

'Have you ever done that,' he asked me, 'fallen asleep in a bedroom where there is a fire lit so that you can lie watching the patterns in the embers? It is quite magical, you wait and see.'

I wish that someone could have painted a picture of the room to preserve it. Jack had begun to teach me about paintings. He showed me Dutch interiors and how the light touched on the man and wife within their home. While the man might display external concerns in the energy of his curls beneath his hat, in his ruffs and the turnover tops of his boots, the wife was stilled in impassive content, her face as smooth and moony and luminous as the oval of an honesty pod.

If not painted, I wish even that our room could have been sealed up completely, around the door frame and everything, like a tomb when we were gone. Then nothing would have been lost: every speck of the dust which was precious to me, the way the morning sun had bleached the wood of the painting desk, the multiple baby plantlets which trembled on the bracts of the parent spider plant.

At least I do not forget; when I close my eyes I find my way around that room as if I had lived there until I was old and blind. There was a nail in the kitchen drawer where I always caught my finger and a bump in the wall plaster by the bed. I used to feel for the bump in the small of my back when I held Jack in my arms and watched him sleeping. I was a devoted watcher, with the same depth of absorption as a mother when she watches her child sleeping, holding her own breath and absolutely still, the better to hear the drawing in of breath by the beloved one.

You could say that my father died because of the Family Allowance. Tragedy should be kept separate from the mundane. If human beings must be eviscerated by grief and loss then they should not be made to have ordinary lives as well. A photograph I cannot bear to look at is that one of the piled-up shoes.

On the third Tuesday of September my mother received an official letter stating that as I was no longer in full-time education she was no longer entitled to claim the allowance for me. I imagine that on receipt of this letter she was very angry. She would have cared most about the accusation of a false claim against her as she sat behind the post office counter, stamping books and disbursing benefits and refusing monies to those who had not signed or dated the correct portions of a form.

My mother contacted Clapham County School. There she was already held in low esteem due to the comportment of Lin and because we had made no response to the letter from Oxford.

My mother would have taken the offensive, maintaining, 'She's been coming into school every day, even if she does travel in sometimes with that James girl.'

But from the school secretary came the reply, 'She has not attended since the end of her O levels. Nor did she come to collect her certificates at Prize Day. We were quite surprised at that, considering she had done so well. I must add that the Head is extremely disappointed to learn that you have not yet replied to Oxford.'

'There must be a mistake.'

'I can assure you that there is no mistake. By the way, if by the James girl you mean Alison, who used to be in Susanna's form, she left us many months ago. The family moved out of London.'

My mother did not challenge me immediately; she waited. She discussed it with Lin and with Ron. Subsequently, when she had discovered where I spent my days and my nights, she sought advice from Lin's boyfriend, who had contacts in the police. At that time the connection and cooperation between established villainy and the Metropolitan Police was very close.

One afternoon I was helping Eunice to re-hang the curtains in her room. Jack had gone to deliver some drawings to a publisher. Eunice had been telling me about her childhood in Leicestershire and her father who had been a railwayman and champion at the pub card game of euchre. Standing on a chair to reach the curtain rail, I looked down at Oakley Street far below and I thought that I saw Ron's car from the driving school. Then I reminded myself that the British School of Motoring had many cars that looked the same, with signs screwed to the roof and identical livery.

I left Eunice to prepare for her evening at the pub on Cheyne Walk. I had begun to feel ill again. I wondered if it might be the weather, unnaturally hot still for the autumn. The city seemed to be radiating back the stale heat trapped all summer; there was a sickly heaviness to it. I decided that I would go home to fetch clothes and return to Jack in the cool of the evening. I did not have a door key and so I telephoned home to see whether anyone was there. I felt better when I saw Julian in Kings Road.

'I don't have to wear uniform, now I'm in the sixth form,' he explained; the boys were allowed tweedy sports jackets and grey trousers instead. 'I'm going for University of East Anglia, I think, they're really good for English, apparently. What about you?'

'I don't know, I haven't been back.'

'What, not at all... why the fuck not, Suse, you're so much cleverer than me, you'll be Oxford or Cambridge for sure.'

'I don't know really, things happened.'

'Are you pregnant?'

'No, of course not.'

'Look, I have to go, my dad's picking me up, but meet me in the Picasso on Friday afternoon, and then we can talk properly and stuff.'

I watched him walk away towards Chelsea Town Hall. The funny haircut feathers bobbed at the crown of his head, emphasising his liveliness and his general open and good-natured outlook upon the world. I never saw Julian again.

When I arrived at the flat my mother came into the hallway and pushed past me to the door I was about to close, slamming it shut. I had seldom seen her so galvanised by energy and emotion. At first I thought it was a joke; it was faintly ridiculous. Then she screamed into my face, 'You dirty, twisted little bitch. How could you? How could you do it, with him? With your own father? Who do you think you are, Lolita?'

With one hand she pushed me in the small of the back towards the living room. They had all arranged themselves there; they had been waiting for me since I telephoned. I could tell by the disposition of the tea cups and the ashtrays. Lin was sitting in the armchair with one leg tucked up beneath her. She was not animated except when she leant forward to flick the ash from her cigarette. Ron was standing up, hitching at the belt on his trousers.

'You're sick,' my mother's voice was quieter now, but with more timbre to it, 'you'll be put away.'

Ron said, 'It's him that should be put away.'

'He doesn't know. He doesn't know that I am his daughter.'

'Don't be so bloody stupid, of course he knows, he's your father.'

'He doesn't know. I lied, about everything.'

Lin made a noise by clicking her tongue and teeth and then smiled in a sneer, which was ugly. 'You can say that again.'

My mother said, 'You've got a damn sight more than lying to worry about, my girl. Now get out of the way, go and shut yourself in your room so that none of us has to look at you, you dirty little bitch.'

'I'll go out again.'

'Oh no you won't. You're going nowhere. You try and leave and we'll have you arrested as well as him. And you'd better tell us when this all started, because if you were under sixteen we'll get him for that as well.'

Again I said, 'He didn't know, he thinks that I am someone else.'

'Like hell he does. He always was a randy bastard but I never knew he was a filthy rotten pervert as well.' She pushed me again.

At the door I paused; I do not know, even to this day, whether it was a child's boast to incite envy or if it was the jealous barb of one grown woman to another. I said, 'It's me he loves. I am the only one that he's ever loved.'

My mother lifted her hand and struck me on the side of my face. In the instant that the slap hit me I saw Lin beyond her. My sister started and blinked at the impact.

In my room I knelt on the floor and rested my head on the bed. To stop the gibbering of panic I tried to think of all the times when I had felt ill or afraid and compare them to the present so that it might not seem so dreadful. I wished that I knew some prayers properly. I wondered if there were words from hymns that would do in place of praying. I thought back to the last time when I had joined in with the singing of hymns, at assemblies in the hall of the junior school, the trees of Wandsworth Common visible beyond the windows.

I wondered when Jack would return from delivering his work. I tried to visualise the old Citroën, nosing round the twilight corners behind Oakley Street where the last flowering shrubs hung over garden walls and dropped petals onto the pavements.

My throat was becoming very painful; it had begun to close and I prayed to God, asking to be so ill that I would be taken to hospital so that Jack and Eunice would come.

At about ten o'clock my mother opened the door. My throat hurt so much that each word I spoke seemed to scrape on it.

'I'll go, you needn't worry, no one will know. We might go and live in France anyway. Please let me out now.'

'I'll let you out all right,' she said.

The road was usually empty at that time of night. From someone's house you could hear the closing theme music for the *News at Ten*. Oddly though, I saw that a knot of people were gathered. There was Ron, with Tommy Sutton and two other men, and Lin and my mother. Ron's security van was parked there too; on its side was painted 'Peace of mind – Priceless'. The two big Alsatian cross dogs were inside, making the van's suspension rock in their frustrated attempts to pace and prowl.

'You take her in with Tommy,' Ron said to Lin.

'Where are we going?' I had little voice to use.

'We're going to sort him out,' Ron replied as he and my
mother got into the van. I thought we must be going to Oakley
Street. I thought what an odd caravan we would make, arriving
in the wide roadway. I wondered if Eunice would look down at us
from behind the curtains we had hung together and whether she
might take me in and hide me. I would ask her if she would try
and help me to persuade Jack to forgive me. I needed to explain
to him that I had had to lie to him because it was the only way
open to me: I could not not be loved by him.

We were not going to Oakley Street. We were going towards
the river, but another stretch of embankment, to The Galleon.
Its bars were already closed. In his rolled-up shirtsleeves, Lin's
boyfriend stood outside awaiting our arrival. The others parked
by the concrete terrace. Ron motioned to Tommy Sutton to park
at a distance, then he and my mother came across and Tommy
and Lin got out and they locked me in.

'Make sure the bloody doors are locked,' my mother said
and walked around the car, trying each chromed handle, yet
not looking in at me. She and Ron walked back to the terrace.
I saw that a wind was blowing from the river, scattering the
contents of the big ashtrays on the terrace tables and making
the collapsed sun umbrellas strain like ship's fittings. Ron took
the undisciplined dogs from the back of the van, they plunged
and yarled on their leads like unbroken horses. The group stood
waiting in a knot by the door of the terrace bar.

The old Citroën turned into the car park entrance. One of
them had telephoned and told him that he must come. I saw him
park near the building, too far and too dark for me to call him,
even if my voice had not been almost lost. Jack got out of his car
and I saw my mother step forward from the group to approach
him. I thought how badly she must have aged in his eyes and I
was almost sorry for her. Although I could not hear the words

I saw from her stance and mannerisms that she was shouting at him. I saw his tall elegant body in the old jersey; at first he seemed only to listen, because he was polite and patient and well mannered. Then he began to respond, using his hands to illustrate his words. More than once I saw him shake his head. My mother spat at him.

Ron and his two companions and Lin's boyfriend advanced towards my mother and father. Tommy Sutton stood back with Lin. Jack was the tallest of them all. I could still see his head, even when they surrounded him. The dogs were so maddened that Ron was holding them by their collars. Then I could not see Jack's head any more because he had fallen.

Within the group some secondary confrontation seemed to begin. One or two were shouting at each other. Tommy Sutton had moved some way away beside the river wall. I saw that the big man in shirtsleeves had bent down to the ground and he must have called Lin to him. Moments later I saw her tear herself from the knot of people and run at Tommy Sutton. The river's breeze was lifting the ends of her clothes and hair. She grabbed at his lapels and for a moment it looked as if they were acting out some wild wind-shrieking playground game and that soon they would turn and spindle into some rhyming chant. But Lin was screaming at him and the wind snatched up and blew me her words, 'For Christ's sake, get her out of here. He's dead, he must have hit his head when he fell. He's dead; get her out of it, for Christ's sake.'

Tommy Sutton drove me to his mother's house in a road off the south side of Clapham Common. All night long I sat in the front living room. There was a polished radiogram and each ornament stood upon a circular mat of pink crochet work. I knew that they would have thrown my father's body into the river; I knew that when the morning came I must go into the water and look for him. I thought that he probably was not really dead. As a young man one summer night he had swum for miles out to sea from the beach at Porthcawl, just to follow the path the moonlight made upon the water, he told me that. I would be able to revive him and make him better. They would not have realised that he had only been unconscious. They were stupid people who did not understand. I must find him and bring him back to life. I knew that when I did the fall itself it would be frightening but that it would be all right because he had gone before me. I did not, ever, want to think that Jack had been afraid. Even normal children do not ever wish to contemplate the possibility that their father could be afraid.

For a time I did not feel sad because I knew that there was not long to wait until I could find him. But then I thought of Eunice and of how she would now be alone on the third floor of the house in Oakley Street. This prospect was so unbearable that I could not contain it. I thought that I must howl out loud but then I saw Tommy Sutton's craft knife on the side table; his hobby was marquetry work. With this knife, as I saw what Eunice would be made to face, I made repeated neat shallow cuts on the back of my left hand in order that I could bear it. The pattern of the cuts resembled pins spilled in the bottom of a workbasket.

I knew that they would say nothing, my mother and Lin and the others from the car park of The Galleon. They would say nothing and they would get away with it, like city people do; they become no more than shadow figures in a modernist painting, no eyes or ears or mouth, seeing and telling nothing, fading back into the concrete angles. And the deceased, John ap Rhys Owen, my father Jack, would be seen as neither the first nor the last, merely one among many who choose to end their life among the drowned dead of the River Thames. The coroner would record him as a man in late middle age with a history of alcohol problems, unpredictable, temperamental, as artists are known to be. The river would have washed away from his body all trace of my anointing of him, early in the morning of his last day. The Galleon's manager, Lin's boyfriend, would affirm that there had been a man, middle-aged and morose, drinking alone in the bar earlier that evening. He might even have amplified his evidence with a description, portraying how the man had snarled in that way that drunkards have if the pot man tries to collect their glass before it is empty.

I saw the dawn come beyond the pink curtains. I got up from the chair in the neat room and left the house and walked to the river. It did not take me long. Few others were about so early. Beside Albert Bridge the sweet dew scent was rising from the Battersea earth as it must have done when all that land was market gardens still. I let myself fall and I did not feel afraid.

But it must have been delirium by then because an hour had passed and I had not moved at all.

Until the very last moments of his life Jack believed that I was what made him complete, he told me so, with a sense of wonder. And he would say, 'Christ, I'm a lucky bastard; I must be the luckiest man alive, to have you. Who would have thought it, at my age.'

He lamented for all the people in the world who would never feel such things. Sometimes there was the air of the votive, the supplicant, in the way that he looked at my face and all of me and laid his hands upon me. Many times, when he had finished making love to me, I had him lying in a state of abandonment, prostrate across my body as if he had fallen down before me. Like the line from the sacrament of marriage, I suppose.

Then, in those last moments of my father's life, people with mob faces contorted into their own caricatures had told him that it was not so. His beloved girl was a liar and much, much worse besides. When she had taken him by the hand she was not leading him into the places of rapture that he, in his foolishness and his vanity, had supposed. The wind-stirred grass was really the moving of snakes and people's eyes were only empty sockets. They heaped him with horror for what he had done. I saw them do it, I watched Jack lift his hands to his head. In a desperate fleeting hope I thought that he was refusing to listen to what they said, that it was just his old familiar gesture of pushing back his hair when it fell forwards on his forehead and that he was about to turn and make his way home to Oakley Street where I would go and find him and we would close the door on all that was in the world outside. But it was not, he was covering his eyes. He was despising himself for what they showed him he had done. I had to see him as he saw himself: damned.

I could not have got him back from that place; probably not ever. Amid his horror and lamentation he would, at some stage, have remembered that first afternoon in the room above Phene Street and the last moment at which he could have turned away from sin.

But when the time of his guilt and shame and mourning was completed, I think he would have patiently and determinedly reconstructed his life, in that same methodical way that he had done before, after the chaos and the drinking.

He would never have touched me again but, when he saw that I could not live without him, I am sure that he would have let me stay on in the room in Oakley Street. He was a kind man. He would not have turned me out and made me leave him completely. After a while he might even have let me kiss him goodnight. And, day by day, month by month, year by year, I would have planned it so that imperceptibly, with each chaste goodnight, my lips could light upon his dry cheek a hair's breadth closer to his mouth.

They took my father's body to the mortuary of St James Hospital. St James Hospital is in Balham, just beyond Wandsworth Common. If I had still been at school I could have looked across from one of the pepper-pot towers to the rooftops and windows of St James.

They must have laid him on something like a cold flat bed. When he was exhausted by making love he was very still in his sleep afterwards. I used to have to listen with utmost concentration to hear the inspiration and expiration of his breathing. If I had been allowed to see my father dead I would have knelt down beside him to try and hear the breath again. I would have watched through the night if needs be and I would have taken his hand and held it to make it warm again. Sometimes, when I leaned over him to kiss him, the ends of my hair would brush across his face and that would wake him or at least make him stir. I expect that they would have closed his blue eyes so I would have kept my eyes closed as well, then we would each be seeing the other only inside our heads.

If I could not have made him warm and breathing again then I would have taken off any clothing I had and lain down beside him and instead he could have passed his coldness into me so that we were both of us become numb. Just before the coldness took hold I think I would have heard him speak to me to tell me that it was all all right. Once in the room in Oakley Street he said to me, 'I hope you know how much I love you, Susanna, because, God help me, I could never put it into words.'

PART TWO

From the very beginning, they gave me a room of my own. The ceilings are high and the paint-work uniformly cream. The bed too is high, markedly raised above the linoleum floor, and in the wall behind it there are metal sockets of various kinds and a call bell. I think that the sockets are for emergency equipment on occasions when I may do myself harm. In the door there is a glazed square with a grid of wire inside it. People observe me through it, sometimes I know when there is a face there, and sometimes I do not bother to notice. There is nobody's face in the world that I want to see but when it is Bonnie Jean I know that she will always smile.

It was easy to become adapted to living here because for the first months I was what Trevor calls very doped up. I slept, or I merely gazed into the foreground space a great deal, dozing with my eyes open. I was conscious of things going on around me only in so far as you notice a fly buzzing against a window pane or a television set in another flat. Therefore, by the time I was more aware of my surroundings and they reduced the dosages, I was already accustomed to this place.

Beyond the window it is south-west London still, but some-where near Tooting Common so I see no familiar landmarks. What I do see are the networks of covered walkways and the external metal staircases. It is an extraordinary work of engineering, this institution. Precisionist painters in thirties America made pictures of buildings like this, although theirs were in the main factories and warehouses, not, I think, mental hospitals. Sometimes I read assiduously on painting and painting styles, sometimes I am unable to – in the illustrative plates just the placement of a hand or the fall of light from a window or the portrayal of the sitter's age can set me off. In the beginning Trevor and the man in charge who conducted my first assessment would ask me why I was so interested in art. I told them that I did not know, I just was.

'I think you do know, Susanna,' said the man in charge.

'Piss off,' I replied and I began to worry at the stripe of dark red stitches up my arm.

I am very knowledgeable now but only in the areas on which I have been able to obtain works of reference. Sister Anna Maria, the nun with the library trolley, does her best but such books are not easy to come by and so there are extensive gaps in my learning. Whole genres must go uncomprehended.

Here in the room in the asylum at Tooting Bec I play a waiting game and so do they, those who have charged themselves with making me better. At first I presumed that they only wanted to cure me of my grief, which was ridiculous, and to stop me cutting my hands and then my left arm. I can tell you that did not work either, the flesh of that limb being quite transformed nowadays. I do not think that my father, who once told me about a man in an American novel who was so obsessed with women's arms that he got an erection just at the sight of bare ones, would be able to recognise it any more. The thing being that when I cut it a lot infections take hold and so now there is considerable scarring, my skin like the moon's surface or an arid landscape of pits and cracks, sometimes flushed and febrile. Human bodies can produce all by themselves the most marvellous tones and pigments, simply by the processes of injury or of sickness. From a bookstall on the Left Bank Francis Bacon once bought an old volume on diseases of the mouth; he recorded that he was entranced by the beauty of the coloured illustrations.

It is only the left one that I cut; I am quite particular about that. At morning break in the brown-painted cloakroom of Clapham County School a third-form girl read out extracts from the teenage magazine *Jackie*. The air was redolent with the smell of plimsolls and cheese and onion crisps. The magazine was a special edition for Valentine's Day; it offered salient facts in heart-shaped frames stating that February 14th was the birds' wedding day and that the Romans chose the third finger of the left hand for the ring because it had the closest connecting communication to the heart. I went home and told Lin but she said how the hell would they have known that.

After a time in the Springfield Hospital at Tooting Bec I came to understand that it was not simply the grieving or the cutting that they are seeking to address. They are waiting for my admissions: for me to admit that I remember what I did, to tell them about it, all of it, and to acknowledge that it was wrong. Good luck to them in their endeavour. I have been here a long time now. Bonnie Jean has saved for and enjoyed a trip home to family in Barbados. The main man from my very first assessment, whom I dislike for his pipe smoking and for other things, has been on a lengthy sabbatical. I hoped that on his return he would eschew our pointless weekly sessions but he did not. His name is Derrick Hearn and you can sometimes glimpse him in his private moments applying a plastic comb to his hair on which, unfashionably, he uses Brylcreem. I sense that he intends to make some sexual advance towards me and to write a paper on my state of mind and deviancy. If he ever did the first, I would harm myself good and proper. I do not know, as I have been sectioned, whether I have any rights to stop him doing the second.

My mother had me committed. On the 14th November 1972 I swallowed the bottle full of sleeping tablets that the elderly GP on Clapham Common West Side had prescribed to stop me banging my head against the wall in the long nights. I took them with some of Ron's whisky which was rather a cheap brand with a golden cap to serve as a measure. After that I opened up my left arm with the carving knife from the wrist to the elbow.

'Ah, it's the flowery scent,' Jack used to say when I had newly applied Diorissimo on leaving work to go to him. 'Come here, come here to me, Susie, and let me breathe it in, breathe you in.' And he would bend his head like a courtier and put his face against each of my wrists in turn and then, lifting my long hair, seek the places behind my ears. Diorissimo is a young girl's scent. I began the cut just at that point on my left wrist that I used to spray. I wonder if the flesh there had held a faint residue of fragrance, like some velvet treasure an old woman has put away in tissue paper. If so, the blood would have washed away all trace of it.

When my mother saw she said, 'I'll have you committed,' and she did.

Unlike the others, Trevor has not had many absences. He works very hard and dedicates long hours to his case notes. Only for a fortnight in the summer does he absent himself; he takes his wife on holiday to Spain, he says it makes up for him not being around much otherwise. This year they both got food poisoning from shellfish. Trevor is plump and earnest and badger-bearded. His appearance is generally crumpled and often in mid-afternoon he attempts to boost his flagging energy levels

with a peanut Marathon bar. He makes weak jokes and to indicate the punchline he gives a snorting laugh within his badgery
beard. He calls all us patients by our first names and he strives to
be our friend but try as he might we know that at the day's end
he will go home and we will not.

I calculate that I am the only one here who does not want to
leave. If anyone asks me where my home is I tell them that I do
not have one any more. Once someone persisted, a dark-haired
woman named Sally who claimed to have been an air hostess
with BEA. 'Where did you used to live then?' she asked.

'By the river,' I said and immediately regretted it in case she
told the doctors and they used it as evidence of my having a
memory after all. I thought she might have been an impostor, a
spy planted to draw me out. Certainly her appearance was a lot
smarter than the rest of us. As though abstracted I rose from the
jigsaw of the bridge at Henley that we had been doing together. I
went to sit on the floor, affecting the hugging and rocking movement which I had seen vacant-eyed others enact until staff bent
down and spoke to them with exaggerated pronunciation, as
they would have addressed themselves to foreigners with little
grasp of English. I need not have worried; next day Sally was
moved on to somewhere non-NHS.

I prefer Trevor to be present during the sessions with the pipe
man but this is not always possible. In one of the interminable
meetings the latter said to me, 'You are a clever girl, Susanna. I
want you to tell me what you have done wrong.'

'I haven't done anything wrong.'

'You did things which were very wrong, didn't you?'

'No, I didn't.'

One of the children on Alison's estate was once challenged,

on the pavement, by a shopkeeper who accused him of steal-
ing. We bystanders could clearly see the item that the boy was
holding behind his back. Escape seemed quite impossible, it was
surely all up for him, the insouciant thief, whose name was
Kevin. But Kevin stood his ground, literally, with planted legs in
school uniform trousers which were grease marked and frayed
above the hem.

'I don't know what you mean,' he said in round blue-eyed
disbelief at such an allegation. He ran some of the words together
as though there were a 'ch' sound at the end of 'what'.

'I don't know what you mean,' I said to pipe man Mr
Derrick.

'Yes, you do.'

His office was on the ground floor, at the building's corner so
that there were two windows. He sat with his back to these.

'We know and you know that the reason you are here, mainly,
is that you had been doing something very wrong, hadn't you?'

At the moment when it seemed most hopeless in the stand-
off with the shopkeeper, thieving Kevin had suddenly flung the
stolen item into the air so that its crude coloured packaging
soared heavenwards in an arc of blue and yellow. Then he ran
like a hound, leaping and jumping and bounding high as the
hero in a nursery rhyme.

'You did something that's not allowed by law, something
that's frowned upon by the medical profession, by the Church,
by society as a whole; it's a taboo.'

'My sister has a scent called that, but it's spelt with a "u"
at the end. Tabu by Dana. I don't like it, personally, it's awfully
strong.'

'What was it that brought you in here to us?'

'An ambulance.'

'Don't be a silly girl, Susanna.'

I stared over at the mantelpiece where there was a pipe rack. I wondered if I really was still a girl, now that I was older and I had cut off all my hair. I used the tiny nail scissors which they had forgotten to remove from the back of my little pink mani-cure set. Bonnie Jean shook her head sorrowfully as she knelt to pick up all the long thick chestnut strands and put them into the paper rubbish bags which they hang on the side of hospital lockers. There was so much that she needed three bags.

'Darling,' she said, 'now why did you go and do a thing like that?'

'...for heaven's sake look at you,' said love-at-first-sight Jack, 'with your long, long hair...'

What possible use was it to me now?

'Admitting that what you did was wrong is the first step towards your recovery, Susanna.'

I concentrated on the carpet, which was blue speckled with black.

'You'll have to tell us, sooner or later, it might as well be now.'

On the desk Derrick man had a shallow glass pen tray filled with paperclips. I opened one out and began prodding my hand with the end of its wire.

'That is called stippling,' Jack explained, showing me how he had filled in a space in a landscape. 'You take a brush, quite a thick soft one, and you move it like this.'

The end of the paperclip was too blunt. I had only just started to bring up blood in the stipples when Trevor got up and came across to me. 'Hey,' he said and gently he took the paperclip away.

'I think we should leave it there today,' he said and he led me away though I knew that grease-headed Mr Derrick did not agree.

ANNE PEILE

That, more or less, is how it goes with me. Periodically I am led to a consulting room, they keep on insisting that I must remember and that I must be contrite, I persist in obstructing their advances. Sooner or later they lead me away again, back to the room where I live all my days and all my nights.

The loveliest nights are the ones when Jack comes to me in dreams. 'Susie,' he whispers to me, 'Susie, are you awake?... I want you all over again.'

I don't have visitors. At first my mother was brought in to attend the psychotherapy sessions. Dr Derrick and a woman asked questions about sex. I said nothing. My mother was expected to go back to my room with me when the hour was over. On the first occasion she unpacked a brightly coloured shopping bag. There was some clothing, a packet of Maryland cookies, a bottle of lemon squash and a book of crossword puzzles.

She put the squash on the top of my locker and said, 'You needn't tell them anything about what happened that night.'

I began to hum; I did not know what the tune was. Perhaps it wasn't a tune, just a rhythm, like the sound of a train.

'Do you hear me, Susanna?'

I made the humming louder.

'You bloody well will listen to what I'm saying to you. They down there...' she jerked her angry head in the direction of the consulting wing, 'they know as much as they need to know about you and this sordid bloody business. Everyone thinks that he probably committed suicide. You dare to give them even an inkling, the slightest idea, that it wasn't that and it will all come out in the papers and in court and everywhere else. You wouldn't want the whole world knowing what a filthy pervert your precious father was, now would you?'

I altered the humming; I thought it was closest to 'For All the Saints'.

'Would you? I know damn well that you understand a lot more than you make out, don't think you can fool me.' She set down the pile of clothing which I knew would smell of cigarette smoke and fried cooking.

The next time she was brought in to a meeting some weeks had elapsed. I must have done something so that they sedated me again. She sat on the edge of a hard chair and when her skirt rode up her crossed legs in their tea-coloured tights she hitched the hem down again on those thighs that she did not shave. They should ask her about that, I thought.

Derrick Hearn's assistant in her crimplene pinafore dress questioned whether I had had any male teachers at school. I remembered Mr Cork for music; a girl with a double-barrelled surname had found a Durex wrapper in the street and placed it in his pigeonhole outside the staff room. I said nothing.

'What about film stars, pop singers, who do you like?'

Who was the man in the film called *Morgan: A Suitable Case for Treatment* I wondered. David Warner, that was right. I had liked David Warner and Terence Stamp. When I was twelve and plump I had sent anonymously a badge saying 'I Love You' in an envelope addressed to Terence Stamp, The Albany, London. When I was sixteen I met a young man in the Chelsea Potter with hair like a yellow lamb; he told me that he was a singer in the chorus of a musical and that he had had his heart broken by Terence Stamp.

'*Noggin the Nog* was good,' I said, 'and the *Pinky and Perky Show*, when the puppets used to jig about to records, that was ever so clever.'

'How many times did you have full intercourse with your father?'

How many indeed, I wondered. A hundred times, a hundred times a hundred times. On more than one of those uncounted, sweet and blissful times, Jack wept. Once it was when he was as high inside me as he could go and yet even so he despaired of his labours. Still he pushed harder and he said that he wished that he could reach my heart that way. Then I felt that there were tears on his face and I sipped them up as though they were spoonfuls and he, excusing or confessing his repeated efforts, said, 'I don't want to let there be any part of you that I have not touched.'

The woman in the sludge-coloured pinafore dress said, 'Well, I can see that you're determined not to be helpful today,' and she and my mother exchanged glances as though they were in the head-scarved huddle at the school gates, sharing anecdotes of maternal and spousal hardship.

Again they expected my mother to return to my room and sit with me a while. I could tell that she would rather not. My head ached from her resenting presence.

'You needn't stay,' I said.

'I'll leave you to them then,' she said, bridling a little. 'There's nothing I can do, obviously.'

After that she left it to two or three times in a year.

Because nobody ever comes to visit me it was unexpected, that windy autumn afternoon when Bonnie Jean, walking slowly because her new shoes pinched, came to tell me that I had a visitor, if I wanted one.

Some half an hour beforehand I had been looking down onto the visitors' car park from my window. I liked watching the brown leaves of London plane and sycamore skittering and chasing after each other across the asphalt. I had noted a woman whose blonde and white hair was lifted at the back with a bar and pin slide. Although this person was unknown to me some quality about her made me feel that I ought to recognise her. Then she was lost to sight within the building and soon afterwards snatches of rain began, hitting the window panes as if thrown in handfuls and making patent shiny the blown and antic leaves.

My premonition about the woman persisted. I wondered if she were some agent of pipe man, another in his chess set of psychologists and analysts and social workers ranked to trick me into talking and to confessing what a deviant was I. I opened my door fractionally and heard the visitor talking in the corridor to Bonnie Jean, who should at that hour be taking her break in the small square airless staff room. 'I'm not a relation as such, just a distant family connection, by marriage.' There was a trace of the north in her voice and a matter-of-fact element; also, she seemed quickly out of breath.

'Well, I'm sure that will be fine and I must say I'm glad to see you, she never has any visitors, this one.'

I heard them coming towards my room and I wanted to escape. I wished that the windows were not locked shut; I would have gone that way if needs be. 'Well, here we are, here's our Susanna,' said Bonnie Jean brightly but looking as though she wished she had made me wash my face and comb my hair.

My visitor was the solid woman with hair of now whitening blonde. It was caught up in a bundle at the back and the pin slide was made of tooled leather. She wore a black coat and glasses with gold wire frames. 'I hope you don't mind if I first sit down,' she said. She seemed noticeably breathless. She took the visitor's chair; I sat on my bed and hugged my knees, which were my paling fence.

'Well,' she said, 'well, it's led me a merry dance, finding you.'

She unwound from her neck a long hand-blocked silk scarf in green and purple which may have been the souvenir of somebody's far eastern travels. On the collar of her blouse I saw that she wore a modern oval brooch in silver and coloured enamelwork but I knew already that she was Olive.

'My name is Olive,' she began, 'Olive Owen.'

I knew that there was nothing I could do but sit and wait. Her eyes were pale blue-grey and her nose tilted up a little, a feature which can be charming in youth and can even make an older woman's face look younger, if she's lucky. If she knows, I thought, if she knows at least I will be able to ask her why she has dropped the first part of his name. I would never do that. 'If one of you had been a boy...' said my mother in her grievances. If I had been Jack's son I could have used the 'ap' as well. I wondered if this visitor woman was going to shout at me. Breathing seemed to be intermittently difficult for her, her doll mouth went into a small straight line and she was silent, looking downwards. I thought she might be noticing the whorls of white fluff that rolled playfully in little billows under my high bed like cartoon mice. Some days I watched them for hours at a time.

'Sorry about that,' she said, after a while, 'I've got this stupid heart thing and it can mean that I get a little out of breath. Do you like art?'

Instead of under the bed she had been regarding the pile of books on my locker shelf.

'Sometimes, it depends.'

'Well, that's good, and perhaps it will make my task easier, in some ways. Do you mind if I call you Susanna?'

Own up now, you might as well, I said to myself. So many secrets and some of them so very beautiful. Jack's hands.

'I am Susie. My name is Susanna but people call me Susie.'

'Well, Susie, there's things I need to talk to you about, if that's all right. I feel that it is important to me, I want to try and get to know you, if I may. I am Jack's wife.'

'Who is Jack?'

'Your father, Susie.'

'I haven't got a father.'

'Yes, Susie.'

'No Susie, no know Susie, know nothing Susie, no things at all.'

I wanted something I could button across my chest. Bonnie Jean came in with cups of tea on a tray. 'Please help me find my cardigan,' I said.

'I thought this might be welcome,' she said to Olive as she set down her cup. I thought that she could not hear me.

'Please help me,' I said.

'It's here, darling, here it is.' She brought it to me on the bed. 'Remember, you can only wear one sleeve. Don't try to put your bad arm in, honey, you know you're not to have anything touching on that now.'

Olive picked up her teacup but her eyes were on the unclothed limb and its bandaging and splint. Bonnie Jean, to emphasise her point about the sleeve, had lifted my left arm gently and laid it down again on the cellular blanket cover. One humid summer night I had played a juvenile, foolery game with the husband of the woman who sat beside me. Unable to sleep due to the heat and to the insatiate lust which even to our own selves was a wonder and a delight, we had done that thing that children do, piling hand over hand, describing an ascending tower in the air. I recall that one of the sheets had been wrinkled and rumpled into a roll, as though someone in a laundry had been wringing it out. 'You win,' said Jack and collapsed himself on top of me.

'Why don't you try your tea, it's very good,' said my father's wife and Bonnie Jean, at the edge of the room, nodded her approval.

'I can't,' I said, 'I can't do it.'

Simultaneously both women must have decided to interpret this as drinking my tea.

Olive said, 'Shall I...' and Bonnie Jean said no, that she had better. To me she said, 'Would you like a pink pill with it, Susie, would that be a good idea now?'

I nodded and some minutes were used up by her administering the tea and the pill during which Olive could not speak to me.

'She's not used to seeing people from outside. Have you come far?' Bonnie Jean, smoothing my head, enquired of my father's wife.

'Quite far, Suffolk, actually, but I am used to the drive, at one time I did it two or three days a week, for work.'

When you were teaching, I thought, at Kingston School of Art.

'Where were you working, then?' Bonnie Jean makes conversation as she chafes my wrist and tells me there, there, now.

'At an art school.'

'Well, there's a nice coincidence, isn't it now, Susanna? This girl is so keen on art, you would not believe, isn't that right, Susanna?'

'I am very cold.'

'All right, feet under the covers then, come on.' Bonnie Jean is immensely patient; whenever she waits for me to complete tasks she stands impassive, with one hand on her chest and the other on her hip until I have done, as though she has all the time in the world.

'Yes, I noticed the books; who have you got there?' Olive leans forward so that she can read the titles on the spine.

'There is nobody else here. I live here on my own.'

'You do seem to like a wide range of work, Susie. It must

be something you've inherited; I suppose you can inherit such things.'

I suspect that she will confront me as soon as Bonnie Jean leaves us alone together. I wonder if she carries a picture of Jack in her head; righteously, holding it up for me to see, like the banner of a protest demonstrator or a statue on a Holy Day. I hope not. Strictly speaking he belongs only to me, she should be told that. I am his one and only, now and ever shall be. But inside I was becoming less pugnacious and more panicky. Silently I began to adjure her, whimpering please do not have a picture of my father inside your head, make it anyone else, a random stranger, the better man you could have married. Please, not him.

Olive, with or without her mental placard of righteous indignation, had got up and was walking around my room. She paused by the window; I might have supposed that she was being considerate and discreet in looking away, in case Bonnie Jean had to perform some personal or undignified task upon me, but she wasn't.

She turned and made her move. 'There's an awful lot I'd like to say to you, Susie, if I may.'

Seeing that I could not get up and run away and save myself from Olive and her head pictures and the awful awe-full words she had stored up to say to me, I did the ostrich thing instead. If you cover your eyes and face with your raised arms it keeps people out quite effectively. If your left arm is incapacitated by bandaging and splint you can still manage somehow with one; it is, after all, a desperate measure.

'Come on, ostrich,' Trevor always says, 'I know you're in there somewhere.'

'I don't think she'll be up to much more today,' said Bonnie Jean.

'I understand. I'll come another day, Susie, if that's all right.'

Sister Anna Maria, the library trolley nun whose eyelids flutter like trapped moths, says that only God can sort things out. So far I do not pray because I could only form the plea to have Jack back, and if God cannot do that then what chance is there that I will ever be able to believe.

That teacher, Mrs Bartlett, who taught the foundation of languages in the first year at Clapham County, devoted one lesson to the role of myths and legends. A mere thirty-five minutes from drilling bell to drilling bell, but I recall much of the content, particularly Herne the Hunter. A being who can turn cows' milk to blood is not likely to be forgotten. 'Some of you might have visited Windsor Great Park with your parents,' she said. 'Herne the Hunter was believed to stalk the Forest of Windsor.'

'You may think you can carry on indefinitely like this, Susanna, but I can assure you that you cannot, we are arranging for you to see a neurologist about your arm, you've caused a great deal of damage to yourself,' says Derrick Hearn.

When I am able to answer him back I can feel again, just for a moment, the Kings Road pavements beneath my feet; and, tasting the sweet angelica trace of Pimm's No. 1, I can flick my long hair and curl my glossy lips and remember that I was once a victor.

'Where do you live, Windsor?' I asked him.

'No, but staff do not disclose their home addresses.'

I nearly said, 'Why, are you afraid us loonies will give you a heavy breather?', but it was only ever personalities like Alison who could carry off such cocky ripostes, and anyway I must try never to let him hear me utter any sexual reference.

When I was taken back to my room there was an envelope lying on the bed cover.

'What's this?' I asked the auxiliary who worked with Bonnie Jean. She said that she was sure she did not know, and taking up the linen she had changed, she left me on my own.

Postmarked Suffolk, it was a large envelope, very like the one that Jack, guilty and elated in unequal measure – probably the ratio being 1:3 – had once despatched from a Sloane Square dawn to his wife in that county. Now that she had tracked me down at last, I saw that Olive, in an elegant symmetry of recriminative impersonation, was having her revenge. Perhaps the content was exactly the same; no accompanying letter; though the guilty lecture notes and carefully annotated slides being message enough for me to understand her meaning, shuttled back across the postal service. I know who you are, I know what you did, shouts the coded message from within his careful script, pause for slide, Jan Steen.

The auxiliary brought me vegetable soup which I knew would taste of the tin. I left it on the tray and she retrieved it at three o'clock. I was pretending to sleep, which was difficult, because I had to curve myself around the envelope that I did not wish to touch.

He had completed the notes for the lecture while I lay and watched him. Although I recovered rapidly from the penicillin episode, Jack's anxieties persisted; he said that I should not return to work.

'I would rather go back,' I reasoned, 'you have to be away anyway, you are giving the lecture.'

'I wonder...' he said, 'I wonder if I could arrange something... maybe... Anyway, your strength needs building up.'

He went out and bought Brand's Essence of Chicken in a jar from the Venice is Sinking chemist. He made me drink cups full of it dissolved in boiling water. I complained incessantly about taking it so that he would fuss over me all the more; in fact I quite enjoyed the taste.

He did not mention the lecture again that evening. During the night I sensed that he had got out of bed and left me long before it was light. I saw that he was back at the desk, arranging the numbered pages and the slides and putting them into a large envelope. The desk lamp illumined his lined face and his upper body. I wish that I could paint a perfect picture of him; otherwise you cannot ever know what a beautiful man he was. When he realised that I was awake he looked across and smiled. 'I've thought of the solution. Olive will be mildly furious but I think that this is the easiest course... and it means I won't have to be away from you until I am sure that you are quite recovered.'

I was feeling that adolescent's need and suckling greed for sleep. I pushed my face back into the pillow. I heard Jack talking to himself. During the day I would have found it amusing, both the fact that he should be doing something eccentric and also the unfamiliar tone of his voice and words: '...do so hate confrontations... really would rather avoid it if one can... so very disagreeable...'

There was an urbane distaste about his monologue; he seemed to have reverted to some fastidious caprice of his youth. Once he told my mother how he had always insisted that his socks for evening wear must be made of black silk. Also, for a short time he had owned a Bugatti sports car and a Dalmatian dog named Jazz.

Some time later I woke again because he was preparing to go out. 'Where are you going?'

'Only up to the post office in Sloane Square, there's an early morning collection from that box. If it goes first thing it won't get held up so she'll definitely have it by tomorrow, the day of the lecture. It will give them time to find somebody else. Have some more sleep, Susie, I will be back beside you before you know it, I promise.'

'No,' I remembered that there had been some reference to Olive being angry and in my fuddled state I thought that she must be at the post office and that she would somehow persuade Jack away. 'Wait, let me come with you.'

He stood watching me with both fondness and impatience while I clumsily pulled on clothes. He strode off down Kings Road as though it was Kinder Scout and my sleep-hobbled limbs had difficulty keeping up with him. I saw that he was elated by the decision he had made; he pushed back his hair and smiled at himself in the silver metal façade of the Chelsea Drug Store, which gleamed in the darkness. Catch him seeing his own reflection and you could be certain he had always known the effect that he had upon women.

'Great stuff, Susie, great stuff... do you know the last time I played truant must have been on Clifton Downs. I had a bar of Fry's chocolate and I planned to hide out for months, like a woodsman.'

'What happened?'

'They'd found me by eleven o'clock in the morning; then I was beaten for it, as usual. I was always getting beaten for something or another.'

We reached the post office and Jack surveyed his package with satisfaction. He had stuck a great many stamps upon it to make sure it met all possible postal charges. When he attempted to post it through the slot in the bronze metal panel it almost stuck.

'Bugger it, cussed thing... I don't want the bloody slides to bend inside...' He shoved the end again and it was received into the box. 'Now then, sleepyhead, we'll just go and sit in the square and make sure the van comes.'

He led me across the road and we sat side by side on a bench like office workers in their lunch hour. I dozed a little and then I saw that a component of the air, filmy as a gauze panel before a ballet performance, was lifting and that the daylight had come. Two pigeons sidled on a window sill above W H Smith's. My head rested heavy on my father's shoulder and from time to time he nuzzled it in an animal mother way. 'Won't be long, then we can get you back to bed.'

As I became a little more awake I was concerned at what an unappealing sight I must look: mascara smudged and my skin like uncooked dough and in general stale. But Jack did not seem to mind at all.

'Okay,' I said and he said, 'Okay indeed,' and leant down and kissed my face repeatedly as though it would tear the flesh of his lips to lift his mouth away.

Surely someone must have seen us there on the dawn seat. Perhaps someone going early to sweep the empty Royal Court stage; or someone flitting a duster over the glass shelves of Mitsukiku where the kimonos were patterned like butterfly wings. If not there, perhaps a resident from the red-brick mansion flats, *soignée* in her dressing gown, the stately widow of some admiral of the fleet preparing her early morning tea tray, cabaret service for one. Somebody must surely have looked down upon Sloane Square so early in that morning of a summer's day and witnessed the tender nature of my father's adoration. I hope that they did, anyway. Sometimes it is a hard burden to think that I am the only one who knows and remembers and understands.

A little later he said, 'Here he is,' and I saw that the van had arrived and the postman had swung open the shiny door and, with difficulty, transferred the package from its wire innards to his sack.

'Done,' said Jack with satisfaction. 'Olive will have that in the morning and we have won ourselves a whole weekend, a whole extra weekend, Susie.'

Back at Oakley Street he said, 'We'll shut ourselves away and we won't even answer the phone. It will be you and me against the world, little one.'

My clothes stayed where they fell. I thought that there was still faint warmth from the mattress. Irresistible both, the heavy draw of sleep beneath me and the weight of my father's body on top of me. 'Now where was I?' he pretends to ask himself, 'where was I... I remember, yes I know...'

Not until it was growing dark outside my room in the Springfield Hospital at Tooting Bec did I realise that the lecture notes would have Jack's fingerprints upon them still. Fingerprints must be transferable; policemen seem to be able to lift them off things all the time. If I held the foolscap sheets against my flesh I would be transposing the ghost of my father's touchings of me.

Olive, whose handwriting was quite like Jack's but rounder, suggested on a single sheet of grey paper that these were things I might like to have and sent also her best wishes. It was not the lecture notes and slides after all. It was bundles of postcards, many reproductions of paintings in rubber bands. Each bundle had been labelled by Jack on a slip of green paper. I set them out on the bed like the formation for a game of patience.

For a long time I sat regarding my father's patient work. I contemplated moving some of the piles around, red nine on black ten, Turner and Spencer, Blake and Rembrandt, Chagall and the Vorticists and Augustus John. Ace can move up. I judged that he must have sorted and wound the bands with his long hands before he ever used those same hands for caressing me. Within, without, and at that dusky skin place where the inner thigh ends; and simultaneously, his dear voice stroking the inside of my head. Years before those caressings he must have sorted and bound this collection; not, though, I think, before he made me. Probably it was during the post-alcoholic period of recovery and rehabilitation from drink, the era when Olive had been his rock. Occupations such as sorting and categorising are invariably soothing and therapeutic. Some years after he made me then; on that September night when he gave me life by convulsing himself out into another woman, just as he had done scores of times before, with many and with any number. Yet the act itself, just that once in his earlier history, was lifted above the ordinary. For on that occasion it was me he created, all unknowing, bringing into the world a girl child; a daughter purely for himself and his delight, earthy coupling to earthly pleasure.

I would never tell Herne the Hunter this but sometimes, when you remember that someone is dead, there seems to be a black space cut out and it is in the shape of their outline. Therefore it is their absence that marks their former presence. Coming to an end is the turn of the card which ensures that there was existence. In that way you can say that there can never be an end because the not being continues, in perpetuity, to prove the being. I could ask Sister Anna Maria. I think that it may be the same as they mean with Jesus sometimes but she might think I am presuming or even being blasphemous. I do not think that she would tell Herne and Co if I spoke to her of dying, so long as I did not make it too personal, but even so I shall not chance it.

If you think that I must mind this existence then I promise you that you are quite mistaken. It was in the beginning that I minded my way of living because, try as I might, I never did belong. Only occasionally odd sections of printed pages caught and blew open the door in the wind and as it banged on its hinges I could see glimpses of beyond.

Then I had those first months in Chelsea, when I went to seek my father, and truly that time was a delight. From Sloane Square to World's End I see it was a Mardi Gras parade, a gorgeous glorious camp and comic charivari: singing, slouch walking and cat calling, doffing and bowing to the pavement crowds. Some days I can recall individuals from that company of players, posing louche and decadent and sooty-eyed in a corner of my mind; or staggering a little on platform soles, making a charming apology for some impolite ailment of depravity. Some of them are brilliantly appointed with stars, these are the little stars of lapel brooches made in diamanté by Yves St Laurent.

And then I did find him, my father. Temptation and what a fall it was. And as we fell together headlong sent we were as immortal as any figure in a painting or on a page who nurses the heart's deep wounds. No absolution for my absolute. Do not ask for credit as a refusal often offends; remember, there was a bargain made.

And so the worst thing that could have happened to me did happen. What did you expect was going to become of me?

In the doldrum afternoons, if we inmates are pacified by heavy puddings or visitors or sedatives, Bonnie Jean and the other auxiliaries like to go to the small staff rest room and watch the drama series *Crown Court*. It is on three times a week and I gather that real people are brought in to be jurors. Sometimes I tiptoe along the corridor and watch through the open door. From behind I see Bonnie Jean, engrossed on the sofa with her companions; behind her white cap her biro is stuck through the small pompom of her bun so that she will not lose it.

One afternoon, peering stealthily from the corridor, I am thrilled to see that Jimmy, the manager from the Great Gear

Trading Company, is playing a part. He seems to be the younger lover of an embezzling woman with a gambling habit. He must have been told to choose his own clothes because he is wearing the Stirling Cooper waisted canvas jacket that he habitually wore in the market. It seems to be a little tight nowadays. Of the two lawyers, prosecution is smooth and silver-haired; defence is stout and pugnacious, bearing the old pock marks of serious acne. Silver-hair is very clever, proving by immaculately tailored arguments just how much learned friend's client's friend actually knew and may, thereby, be implicated.

I am inordinately proud of Jimmy's performance but then I have a pang of sadness because there is no one I can nudge and tell of my acquaintance with him. I went back to bed as pompous notes of music announced the closing credits.

I have not grown fat again; strangely, you would think that I would have done. I have very little exercise and my metabolism must be slowed by all the sedatives they feed me. Nor do I suffer from tonsillitis any more; now that I have no wish to speak with anyone I have all the voice I could want. I asked Trevor why. 'It's probably all the antibiotics we have to zap you with, to stop you giving yourself septicaemia once a week, else it's your age, you've just grown out of it maybe.'

'What would happen if I got septicaemia?'

'You'd probably have to have your arm cut off.'

I smiled.

'I'm not joking, Susie, I am serious.'

'I know you are.'

If they have to take my arm away I will yet be able to feel it. I have heard that happens to people who have limbs amputated. It will be the absent presence again. Sorrowing for the absence is the only way to hold on to the presence. How stupid must they be to think that they can stop me in any of what I do. Anyway, even if I wanted to I could not, there was that pact I made.

I do take some exercise. I walk in the pleasant grounds of this, the Springfield asylum, formerly workhouse, at Tooting Bec. There are large flower borders in the way of a municipal park. Someone goes to great trouble to label all the plants with both their Latin and common names beneath. One of my favourites is Alchemilla mollis, brackets, Mary's Tears. And sure enough, after a shower of rain, drops are held in clear sheer beauty within its soft green leaves. *Lacrimae rerum*.

'Translate this passage for me,' said the Latin teacher whose name, to the deep disappointment of Alison James, did not appear in the A listings of the London telephone directory. 'It's an important one to know and it often turns up in the scholarship exam paper. You need to be familiar with it.' *Sunt lacrimae rerum et mentem mortalia tangent.*

'The tears in what?' I asked her – in things, circumstances, deeds, possessions, facts... But, 'You choose,' she said, so sure was she of my ability and my judgement. I am very sorry that I let her down. That day I chose deeds; now I would choose things.

There is a young gardener. He has close-cut dark hair like toy plush and a perfect sun tan. On hot days he removes his shirt, he has the narrowest hips in his washed blue button-front Levi jeans. I am sure that girls admire him very much. When I know that he is out working I keep away so that he does not have to see how ugly I am.

Bonnie Jean, finishing the plum from her packed lunch, says, 'Time to freshen yourself up, darling.'

It isn't, because it is early afternoon, not the hour for morning or evening ablutions.

'Am I going to get a visitor again?'

'Apparently, she telephoned, Mrs Owen, is it, Olive? Face, come on,' she wipes across it firmly with the flannel in her small strong hand.

I live my life in the passive subjunctive. Mrs A explained it one day, arranging a special extra lesson for me during her morning coffee break.

Olive has brought a canvas holdall; she puts it down and it sits and stays on the linoleum like an obedient dog. 'How are you, Susie?'

'Okay.' In fact I am afraid. I fear the confrontation she will have with me but worse than that, she will drag things into the light. I will have to remember and worst of all there will be noise and alarms and notes taken and I will have to admit that I remember to Herne the Hunter. Better if she would strike me and stone me.

The bag must contain garments that I left in Oakley Street so long ago; a pair of vintage jeans, shipped in one of Uncle Herm's container loads, musty yet astute; a T-shirt patterned with stars. Olive puts to one side the batik print scarf which must still be warm from her powdery pale neck and flaps her face with her hand to cool it. Sometimes Jack used to pick up some article of clothing I had just removed; the first time I thought he was going to tell me off for being untidy, but it was so that he could cradle it to his face or chest like a kitten. It's all right, I tell myself, I am cunning, we know that; I am expert at hiding my secrets within secrets, I always was. In the wash bag, my family's present to me at Christmas, I collect the bedtime tablets. I have a substantial quantity saved up inside the pastel cotton wool balls, pink and yellow, white and blue. I manage it rather cleverly, holding the tablet inside my cheek and letting the nurse witness me in the action of swallowing, grimacing and twisting my mouth with obvious distaste. Someone in the Chelsea Potter told me I had BB lips. I asked a boy I knew what it meant and he explained, Brigitte Bardot, and then he said, 'You have, too.' When the medicine trolley has moved on I slide from bed and add it to my cache. It will be more than sufficient unto the day.

'That's good, I hoped that we could talk a bit today, if that's all right.'

If it was my clothes in the holdall they may not have been laundered since. There would be traces of me and of my father on them. Sometimes semen smells like mushrooms, I observed. 'Yes,' said Jack, 'yes, I suppose it does a bit.'

Olive said, 'Susie, tell me to mind my own business if you like but why exactly are you in here?'

'I've done stuff. Sometimes I hurt myself.'

Both solicitous and lascivious. 'Does it hurt you when I do this to you?' my father inquired and probed. 'Does it hurt you, Susie?... Tell me if it does, best beloved, and I will stop but it's... er... it feels awfully good...'

There is a scale of hurts and pain; the worst not necessarily those experienced physically. You were old enough to have known that for yourself, Jack, and by the way it barely registered, amid all my joy at your enjoyment.

'Do you remember anything about your father, Susie?'

'I don't remember anything, ever.'

'Did you get the postcards?'

'I don't know. Have you been on holiday?'

'I've come to talk to you about your father,' she said, 'my husband, Jack. Perhaps you know of him as John.'

'I know no Johns. You sent me a lot of postcards, in the big envelope.'

'Yes, I did, it seemed right that I should send them to you. Susie, I felt that I needed to talk to you, about Jack, and to sort things out. You see, they've found that I have this heart problem; it may mean nothing, I may go on for years, but whatever happens, I don't want to leave unfinished business, not like Jack did.'

I am so good at being Mistress Crazy, sometimes I roll my eyes and I fancy that I resemble Judy Garland, crisis stricken, in *The Wizard of Oz*. That was a film my mother lauded. She took me to a special showing at the Granada, Clapham Junction. I did not like to tell her that I found it terrifying. It was something about the quality of the colour, I think, also the amateur costuming of that inept triumvirate, straw, tin and up-on-hind-legs lion; had they been slicker then perhaps they would have seemed less sinister.

'I think I told you, it's been a merry dance, trying to find you. He always believed that you were in Australia, you see.'

Not always, Olive, not quite always, was it?

'Who did?'

'Your father – that is, my husband, Jack. My solicitor has been helping me to trace you. He found your sister, Belinda, first of all...'

'I haven't got a sister.'

'Susie, I think you have.'

'There is Sister Anna Maria, she is the nun with the books on wheels.'

'No, Susie, you have a relative, a sister named Belinda. I gather she was quite anti, she did not want any contact made at all, apparently she told my solicitor so in no uncertain terms... anyway, we carried on looking and then we found you. I'm glad that we did, Susie, there are things I need to tell you, if you'll let me.'

'You could tell me anything and I wouldn't remember. I don't have a memory, that's really why I'm here.'

'Susie, it might help us both if we could talk about him.'

I shook my head rapidly; it was difficult for her to decide, I expect, whether I was shaking my head or shivering. Certainly my teeth were chattering.

'Susie.' Olive had placed her hand upon my right hand on the bedcover. 'Susie, I know it's all very difficult, I know that only too well...'

The trouble is that I am too good at this Mistress Crazy lark. I forget sometimes what I know and what I cannot tell and what I cannot know; there are occupied rooms and filled cupboards in my mind, all quite tight shut. Once upon a time there was so much space to spare within, all that was accommodated there being the tiny ammonite curled form, with buds for limbs, of that baby my sister had killed. Nowadays we are full to bursting in these places and I must tell myself to be sure not to lift the latch for fear of what falls out. Jack told me the rhyme his mother used to chant to him:

> *Lift the latch, peep in,*
> *Open the door, walk in,*
> *Take a chair, sit by there,*
> *How are you today, sir.*

Full to overflowing with things, circumstances, deeds, possessions, facts... If ever they all come tumbling out I can tell you it will surely be a flood. Mind yourself, do.

I am of course to an extent crazy but not in my entirety, not so far as I lead them to believe I am; only in the way of one who, both blessed and fallen, bides their time in purgatory. But now I must be tired so that I misunderstand what my father's wife is saying because I am sure with firm press of kindness on my hand she said that she was sorry to tell me that he was dead. Mind yourself. Or did she only say that she was sorry that he was dead.

We sit for a while in silence and with what serendipity do I remember Jimmy and his day in court and that suave barrister character with his ruses. I see that I must establish whether she knows all of it or some of it and that I must be ready, gauging how she will frame her accusation. How high will she construct the arguments for my guilt? She has let go of my hand, which may mean her opening gambit is imminent. I think she is too solid, too practical to shout and make panache with her gown. I wish that she would kill me and make it simpler although I have somewhere for forgetfulness appointed and I do not want it to be in this place instead. She is clever at disguising how much she must hate me. Perhaps her next ploy will be simply presenting my guilty Kings Road *fait accompli* garments – exhibits one and two, patterned with passion spent. Nowadays, given the glittering and over-stimulated transience of that happy thoroughfare, they would for sure be hopelessly out of fashion, perhaps almost ready to come round again on the carousel. In the end I can bear the wait no longer.

'What is in that bag?' I asked her.

She looked up as from a regretful daydream. 'Oh, I'd forgotten that, it's books, art books, I thought you might like to have them.' She fetched the bag to my bed and laid out upon it half a dozen works of reference. 'All Jack's, of course. I am moving soon, so I have been sorting out,' she said. 'Years ago, you know, he often used to say I wonder how they're getting on, those little ones of mine.'

'Little one.' I said.

'What?'

'Nothing.'

Nothing at all, Olive.

'Where are you moving to, London?'

'No, not London. I am moving down to Cornwall, to St Ives. I am going to set up a gallery with a friend. Actually, it will be half gallery, half café, people will be able to sit and have coffee while they browse. At the house in Suffolk we have a big old outbuilding, we always talked about turning that into a gallery, your father and I, but somehow we never got round to it.'

'What will happen to your house in Suffolk?'

'I have sold it, Susie. A family with young children will be living there; it is the sort of place that needs a proper family, really, with the garden and so on.'

I am incarcerated in my cream-painted room and within that room my left arm is incarcerated even more, in its matching cream-coloured crepe bandaging and appliances. There seems to be no part of it I can get at, worry and fret over it as I might. Olive says, 'Why don't you look at the books for a little while, Susie, I'm just going to step out for a moment.'

I know that she has gone for Bonnie Jean; they like each other, those two, I am glad. I can hear them talking outside in the corridor. Olive thinks she might have distressed me by talking of the house move, but if so she makes no sense, because her reason for visiting me is surely to cause me distress. Perhaps she does not plan to do it alone, she may intend to have Derrick H in on the denouement, even my mother too, some ghastly sisterhood of women wronged.

'Certainly it won't do for her to become too attached to you,' says Bonnie Jean.

Yet I do not think that Herne the Hunter is aware even of the two visits, let alone that the visitor is my father's wife. If Bonnie Jean or one of the other auxiliaries ventured to tell him that a visitor had come to see me he would not have bothered to listen. He, as the consultant, sees himself as far superior to the ancillary staff, mainly female; he considers them mere foot soldiers. And so they are, the poor bloody infantry who cope and comfort and clean us; dodging the missiles and foul language and cadences of weirdness that we inmates hurl at them. Their efforts are infinitely more valuable than anything he could do and yet he would never deem their observations worthy of his regard. But can you just imagine the lines on which his stupid brain would run if he did know about Olive, what normalising familial tableaux his dirty mind would pretend it was inventing and favouring?

Just suppose, Susanna, just suppose you had presented your-self on the marital doorstep in Suffolk instead, one chilly after-noon of early spring. They would have taken you in, Mr and Mrs Rhys Owen, no doubt about that. They would have assumed responsibility for you; ensured your education – school and uni-versity – your pastoral care and a wholesome diet. In a matter-of-fact way Olive would have sounded out your knowledge of menstruation and of boys. They would have encouraged you to sketch and to join a local Woodcraft unit and taken you on continental camping holidays. Jack would have expected you to be bored but polite when he expounded his long-term plans for the asparagus bed. Probably he had an old ex-service duffel coat hanging by the back door. On chilly mornings he would have worn it when you and he walked into the village to fetch things for Olive. It would have hung loose and gawky on his frame and, because he was in the sole and proper role of parent, you would have wished that he had instead a sheepskin jacket or fawn car coat, like other fathers did. When you were installed at Oxford they would have travelled down periodically to take you out for meals and express their pride in you. And, when you had flu, Susanna, tucked up in your bedroom in the eaves, Jack would have brought honey and lemon in a pottery mug to your bedside table, having first knocked discreetly upon the thumb-latched ledge and brace door. There you lie, propped on pillows, the demure, picot and gingham pyjama'ed daughter of John ap Rhys Owen, ΛRΛ. Your father would not have presumed to stay, Susanna, nor to sit on the end of your bed, chatting middle-aged pleasantries in his sea green cardigan until you can bear it no longer and, reaching forward in some overarching ache of love, you take hold of him and with your soft mouth you drown him well and truly.

How carefully Olive frames her words when she returns. I wonder if people try harder with the spoken word, now that there is television. Do we hope that the conversation will be timed and perfect, pit pat, pit pat, each side keeping to the script within a set transmission time? She picks up the sumptuous volumes and sets them on my locker top.

'What about friends, Susie?' she says. 'Are there friends who would come in and see you?'

I like Olive. I want to oblige her and so I try to imagine friendly visitors that I could have. First I conjure up Barry French the painter in the corridor; he is wearing his baker-boy cap and doing the impersonation of the Dustin Hoffman character in *Midnight Cowboy*. He used to do it on the zebra crossing by the Markham Arms to annoy the waiting drivers. 'I'm walking,' he would shout, 'can't you see that I am walking...'

Beyond him I can see Alison James with that Afghan hound articulated lope she used to do; her blonde curtains of centre-parted hair and her bony legs which she never intends should look so elegant. Alison ignores limping Barry and says to me, 'Christ's sake, girl, you don't want to end up in here, do you?'

I do not attempt to envisage Julian; he was that boy I used to know. For a time I think I had another friend, a woman that once played cards with me.

'I don't have any friends just now. You mustn't think I mind though, because I don't.'

What an irony, what a pity that you didn't do that. It is Derrick Hearn, muscling in again with his dreams of rural Suffolk and its pre-lapsarian vegetable gardens. He should have heard what the women at the Nine Elms wash baths used to say about certain perpendicular vegetables. But what a pity, he persists. Do you not wish it had all turned out differently?

What a pity, Dr Derrick Mr Hearn the Hunter, what a pity it is that you are so stupid that you miss my point. Did I not say, right at the beginning, that in none of this did I ever know any doubt? I knew what I was doing, you can be sure of that.

'Susie, I will try and come again, before the move. There are some more books, if you would like them.'

It was during the night that I realised what was confusing me. Perhaps not that night, it could have been later in the week or month. My father Jack was a kind man and, in talking to me of his death, his widow had seemed to be a kind woman. Actually I would not have objected if she had presumed to hug me. Almost, I wish that she had. If Olive had hugged me we would have formed some kind of human chain, reaching back to Jack alive and the last time he had held each of us in his arms. I wonder when that was, for her.

I know well the very last time that Jack held me in his arms. It was during and after making love to me on the morning of the day he died. When he was done with gasps and moans he trailed his fingers over me at his leisure and called me his sweet thing and his dear girl and his beloved. Some in my circumstances – I mean only other lovers – might say that if only they had known it was to be the last time they would have been more ardent, more generous, more tender. I, of course, have no need to say any such thing. If I seem arrogant then I maintain that it is permissible and perfectly excusable. For I know that my responses to my father-lover could not have been bettered, ever.

Anyway, the point is, that I should try to remember her exact words: was Olive sorry he was dead or was she sorry to tell me that he was dead because if it was the second she could not know that I had known him, at the end?

I have begun to wait for the post to come, in case Olive should send me something else. I know that it is always one of the grey-coated porters who distributes internal and external mail around this institution; sometimes you can see them crossing the car park with a whole trolleyful. Once I was misguidedly excited by the arrival of a large envelope for me. I should have known immediately that the backward-sloping blue biro could not be from Olive but I wondered if someone had done the address on her behalf and so I worried that she had been taken ill with her heart. Then I recognised the handwriting as Ron's. Bizarrely, he must have included me on the mailing list for the new venture which he and my mother had launched, a driving school of their own. They had called it the Abba School of Motoring; presumably that was in order to be the first entry in the telephone book listings. They had had printed promotional desk calendars in red and black. It was amusing for me to imagine the earnest efforts of Ron over his list, detailing the addresses of other tradespeople, innocuous, decent and honest premises – wallpaper shops and repairs garages and post offices, then me, wayward deviant daughter of his co-habitee woman friend, c/o the mental hospital.

On another occasion I made a grave error of judgement: while the porter had sloped off for a smoke I went into the corridor to scan his abandoned post trolley but Herne the Hunter, unbeknown to me, was lurking in the ward office. 'What do you need, Susanna?' he asked me.

'Nothing from you, at any rate,' I said and returned to my room, but my heart was beating fantastically fast in case he had guessed the object of my interest. I lay down and hid my face under the cover, fearing that he would follow me. I knew that he had seen me startled by his sudden appearance and he might think that thereby he had gained some advantage, some Achilles chink in my protective armour. I shut my eyes inside the dark warm tent of the blanket.

'Look at the picture on the wall behind her.' I sit at the painting desk and Jack leans over me, pointing at the Vermeer on the page. On his breath I can smell the Demerara sugar, two spoonsful, that I stirred into his coffee for him.

'There are symbols in that picture: the sea is said to represent love and the ship is the lover, therefore we can suppose that the letter she is reading is from her sweetheart or husband, who is a sailor away at sea.'

That is almost the skipping rhyme and the singing game, blown on the breeze up and over the high wall of the infants' playground between the Commons:

> A sailor went to sea sea sea
> To see what he could see see see
> But all that he could see see see
> Was the bottom of the deep blue sea sea sea...

You never wrote me a letter, Jack. You told it all into my ear instead. I wish you had written me something, even if you had just left me a note pinned to the door. Some scrap for me to hold on to. Gone to deliver drawings, back soon, please wait. Love Jack. Gone to Fitch's for more inks. Love and kisses Jack. Susie, I love you so much that you cannot and will not live without me, signed Jack. Like some Renaissance polymath you have stripped my veins and turned them inside out but you never recorded it on paper. You did not even leave me so much as a scribble in a margin. Nothing.

If I had left you for a while, if I had agreed to go to Oxford, would you have written to me then, I wonder? And what would we have said to each other, in the mail? Would you have repeated on paper what you murmured to me in all the sweet long nights and vowed in the aching early mornings when sometimes, to draw out that exquisite anticipation, you stilled yourself in the action of entering me, like someone paused to listen. And how would I have replied to you? Cramming into a small blue envelope what huge words of love to be carried like an eggshell across Oxford's hard cobbles to the pillar box.

It is not fair that he left me no testament. He should have known to do so, he was older and he had seen far more than I have seen. If we had been allowed to go together it would not have mattered but the greatest unfairness is that I must stay such a long time in a waiting place, knowing that the evidence of he and I will be lost for ever. With pity for myself and state a lump swells in my throat. Jack used to nearly choke me sometimes, when he came into my mouth. I never got to like that very much but to see my father in his ecstasies was thrill enough for me... And this now, this waiting place, it is my punishment of course. I knew, when I sealed this bargain, that I would have to make atonement. For now there is nothing to do; I must keep silent and suffer.

Yesterday was very bad. No especial reason, just that some days the passing of time is more difficult for me than others. Bonnie Jean is very good, she senses when it is going to be worst. She settles herself on a chair beside my bed and she has the knack of looking elsewhere while she sits and holds your hand; by pretending that she is not concerned, it makes the episode seem less serious.

Before she went home she gave me a pink pill and made me take it with Bournvita. It was only four o'clock in the afternoon but she said that it would be better if I could settle myself down early. For a while I did but then I had dreams and the elderly man from the next wing was very disturbed. Before I saw him I always used to imagine that his appearance must be fantastical and melodramatic, as poor howling Mrs Rochester is envisaged; but then I did see him one day and he was just an ordinary old London man in a vest. He might once have been a boxer. In a second-year English class we debated who was the most frightening, everyone else said the wife, that it was obvious, I was the only one who thought that pipe-smoking Grace Poole was worse.

It was a long time before anyone came, I had the light on but it was very harsh each time when I opened my eyes between banging my head on the metal bed end. It was a man that came;

more often it is men at night. They have a highly developed technique of making you swallow medication when they are in a hurry. Farm animals are handled like that. His colleague was shouting at him from beyond the swing doors at the end of the corridor. I lay down because I knew that he needed me to do so. As he backed hurriedly out of the room, he lifted his hand in a halting gesture. 'Stay where you are,' he said, 'just stay where you are.'

I tried but the howling of the Bertha Rochester man was like a wild animal and I could not block out the indignity of the situation that he – who had once been fearless and strong, a bragger and a brawler – must now be enduring.

Perhaps there was a change of shifts because next time it seemed to be two different orderlies. One said, 'Jesus Christ, she's blacked her bloody eyes now.'

They brought more medication, this time in a syringe. I knew that it would be responsible of me to explain that I had had something earlier but my tongue was woolly and my throat was sore from weeping or some such that I had done. Anyway, to me rehearsal for oblivion is always welcome.

Knock-out one combined with knock-out two proved most efficacious. I was unconscious for I do not know how many hours or even days. Subsequently I was in a state where I could hear but not speak and feel. I could not move at all, I could not even lift my eyelids, though these may have been made the heavier by the bruising of them. At one point someone said, 'Check her signs for me, will you? I'm not sure what I can find.'

It felt as though I was bound to the bed and also weighted down so I knew that I was unable to respond. Once I wished that I could reassure Bonnie Jean for she sounded most anxious.

The next time I was aware of voices it was her again but she was saying, 'Our Susanna's not with us today, I'm afraid, such a pity, when you've come all this way again.'

'What has happened to her face?' asks Olive.

'She hurts herself, my dear, they do that, sometimes, bang their heads, cut themselves, you can't always get to them in time.'

Sounds went in and out like tuning the old wooden wireless we once had; I liked the names on the dial, Hilversum, Budapest, Eireann...

'Will she get better?'

...Munich, Moscow, Allouis, Luxembourg...

'Who's to say, my dear? Not you or I, anyway. Would you like to stay a while, sometimes it will bring them round, if they're aware of someone in the room with them. Here, take this chair and I'll fetch us some tea, I was going to sit with her anyway.'

Olive must have been sitting watching me. Her same eyes would have watched Jack many times. In physics they explained about sight with pinhole cameras but I did not understand. She would have looked at him without even seeing him, because she expected him to be there. I always saw him. Ever faithful I watched and learned and I knew every nuance of his expression, not even the smallest muscle of his face would tic without me recognising immediately whether it was bliss or close to bliss, fatigue, concentration, anxiety or memory, or that transcendental, contemplative state of perfect love which I, blessed one, was able to induce.

I heard the cups and saucers. 'It's a good thing, I think, that my husband never saw this,' said Olive.

'So you're a widow then, is that right?'

Bonnie Jean has been married for twenty-six years. Her husband's name is Leo; they are very content. Sometimes when she is changing the dressing on my arm she talks of their home life and I glimpse it as though through the yellow lighted windows of houses seen from a train. The worst row they have ever had was over the subject of trade union membership. Their two children are grown up and making their own way. On Friday afternoons Leo comes to meet her after work to help with the heavy shopping.

Now, the vicarious shiver indulged from the place of safety, Bonnie Jean wants to know how someone else's husband was taken away. 'What happened, had he been ill?'

'No, not at all, it wasn't that.'

There is a tone in women's voices, even solid women, which comes when they are talking about something which is difficult for them; it is querulous, almost, but paradoxically that querulousness is an indication that they are being brave, rather than timorous.

'There was some sort of accident; at the inquest the possibility that he... that he had killed himself arose... Suicide, you know, suicide is the ultimate form of violence. I hadn't realised that before, it was just a word, albeit with dreadful connotations for those concerned. But when it was being said, about my own husband, I could see then that it is the most extreme form of violence...'

I still cannot speak or move but going through the motions of attempting either action is so effortful that it renders me unable to hear. It acts upon my ears like being underwater. When I next can listen I know that they are looking at me, with my funny bits of doll hair and my damaged eyes. I had a doll once, bought for me unexpectedly by that Clapham landlord. I called her Marigold and to my great regret I cut off her lovely yellow nylon hair during a dressing game; I tried to fix it back again by plaiting it in but it was not a success.

'I must say I've wondered if there was always some flaw, something wrong, and if so, whether it could have been passed on to Susie.'

'Did he show any signs before, of being disturbed?'

'None. He was in a bad way when we first met, but that was alcohol, mainly. Once we got through that, no, not at all. Not the easiest of men, he had his dark side, but nothing untoward.'

'And were you happy?'

'Yes, well I thought so, most of the time. He liked to be alone a lot; I stayed in our house in Suffolk...'

I expect that one of the first things that the father of the new family will do is fix up a swing, on one of the apple trees.

'He used to live and work in London, during the week. In that last year of his life, that's when things changed.'

'Why so?'

'Another woman, inevitably; entirely unoriginal, I know, but my goodness, he had it bad. I used to watch him when he came home at weekends, when he didn't know I was looking, and I used to think my God, Jack, one of us is headed for a fall. I tried warning him, gently, but it didn't make any difference.'

'Did you ever ask him outright?'

'No, I never did. I thought about it sometimes, especially when he behaved very badly and let people down because he was so obsessed. Do you know, one Sunday we had gone out to a special lunch with some very dear old friends, it was their twenty-fifth wedding anniversary. We'd only just started and suddenly he jumped up, like a man possessed, and said he had to go; no apology, no explanation, he jolly nearly ran out of the restaurant...'

So, my father's wife describes events earlier in that day; the other occasion on which I saw him weep. This was by far the worse; you may know that sobs issuing forth from a grown man sound quite dreadful. I, all unaware and humming a song from Ali's radio, had climbed the stairs at Oakley Street in a haze of Diorissimo and anticipation, the tips coins weighing down my pockets. Jack had given me a key and I did not expect him to be back but he was waiting in the doorway of the room and he snatched me as if from danger at a cliff or platform edge. Then I realised that he was sobbing and he told me that he had thought that I was never coming; he said, 'Oh, Susie, thank God,' and he tilted my face as though he expected to see some sign or device of bad tidings inscribed there in magic writing, and then again he hugged me to his chest and was sobbing the more so. I felt that I was ill equipped to deal with this adult grief. Lacking any appropriate stock of conversational phrases I did the only thing I could think of which might give him comfort: I began to undress. Expiating his sobbing and his sorrow he pushed me very hard that afternoon, bruising me quite markedly, there on the teatime bed. I accommodated and indeed encouraged his brutishness because I felt that it must be reassuring for him to do it that way. As he finished he might have been turning himself inside out. Afterwards he apologised; not for his ferocity, but for his earlier comportment, so really he was saying sorry not to me, but to Olive and to the old and dear anniversary couple friends.

'God, what a stupid cuss I am. There I was with half a bloody avocado in front of me like a bar of soap and this blind panic seized me... I had this awful presentiment, I just had to get back to London to see...'

'What did you think had happened?'

'I thought... er... I thought... I got this idea into my head that you had decided to call it a day... that you wouldn't be here any more...'

'But I promised you.'

'People break promises, Susie. Christ, I should know that better than anyone...'

'I don't,' I said and then the kiss that I gave him was almost vicious.

'I don't.'

'It's all right,' says Bonnie Jean, 'she's dreaming, that's all.'

'The funny thing was, apart from the times when he let people down because of it, I wasn't angry at all. Well, I was a bit, with myself, for not knowing sooner, but I wasn't angry with him; I couldn't be, you see, because he was so absurdly, ridiculously happy. I couldn't find it in me to begrudge him, I did care for him, after all and he was, I don't know... transformed by this affair.'

In the Chelsea Potter, when Barry French was describing some supreme moment of pleasure, he talked of being translated. Bonnie Jean must have brought them biscuits to share from the big red Family Assortment tin; for a while I listened to crunching.

'And did you know her, this woman?' Some determination transmitted itself from my brain through my central nervous system and my hand twitched. Bonnie Jean leant across and patted it.

'No, I'm still not sure who she was...' Her voice trailed into a dreaminess. 'But, my God, he must have loved her...'

For a few seconds I sensed Olive regarding my marked face and my bits of ruined hair and her gaze was making them precious again. Fleetingly, during those few seconds, I believed that she knew and was recognising me for what I was to my father and as she held out her arms to me I gave myself up and both of us were glad for knowing.

'And do you think that there was some connection here?'

'How do you mean?' Olive's tone snaps back sharply from its dreamy state.

'I'm sorry, I didn't mean to pry.' Bonnie Jean begins to stack up their cups and saucers.

'No, no, I know that you didn't, and it is a question I have asked myself, that and other things. I just don't know. I did try to find answers. As soon as I felt able to face it I went to the house where he lived during the week, I thought that the people who knew him there might be able to cast some light...'

As surely as if I were able to open my eyes and look, I know that outside the window the sky and the line of treetops have lurched sickeningly and wildly as when the liquid in a snow storm globe is tipped. It is vital that I muffle what she is saying. I do it with the song, which somewhere Jack is singing; he is humming, not in tune, over some task. Shoes. He is polishing the old brown shoes with the brush and the Cherry Blossom Shoe-shine from under the sink, kept beside the medicinal Spanish brandy... *They can't take that away from me... oh no they can't take that away from me...* He sings louder over the rhythm of the vigorous brushing but I can hear chair legs scrape upon the linoleum as Bonnie Jean pushes it back against the wall. I want him to sing louder still so as to block out the light that Olive has seen cast. But I am safe after all.

'But there was no one... there had only been two of them left in the house, old-time tenants with controlled rents. Once Jack was gone, the landlord was quick to persuade the last one out and sell, it was such a valuable property, you see... so there was no one I could ask, no one who would have remembered him. He lived a very solitary life in London.'

'A bit like a monk's cell,' says Jack as he opens the door that first night before he falls headlong into my eyes.

'Maybe it is just as well not to know,' says Bonnie Jean and Olive says that maybe it is, and as she departs she pauses to pat the cover of my bed with its smooth white icing sheet.

Periodically Trevor tries a new tack, especially when I have had darker days. Herne never does, he just worries at old ground mercilessly; probably he even bores himself. But Trevor, dedicated and optimistic, feels it incumbent upon himself to ponder new strategies and potential for us inmates. He might have been a curate in a deprived parish, wearing a chunky wooden cross and running a youth club.

'How do you envisage your life after you leave here, Susie? What would you like the future to be?'

'Don't know.'

'Come on, Susie, what do you want?'

What I want, Trevor, is to let my head sink, with a sigh, upon my father's chest so that at last I can safely go to sleep again.

> *When I lay me down to sleep*
> *Fourteen angels watch to keep...*

I can listen for the rise and fall of his breathing and be lulled and comforted by the little bits of sweetheart words he murmurs to me, scraps of coloured ribbons, as we drift towards our rest. *Someone to watch over me...*

'Will you have ambitions for yourself, do you think? Are there things you hope to do? You could have gone far at school, we know that.'

'What do you most want in all the world, Susie?' Side by side in the bed in the room in Oakley Street we lay, Jack and I.

'You,' I said.

'You're very sweet.'

His arms and my arms were straight down at our sides. I was holding his long hand and I closed on it very tightly, pressing hard on the bones.

'I mean it, Jack,' I said.

He turned on the pillow to look at me. It was only the third time that I had been to bed with him. As he comprehended the strength of my conviction his eyes were for a moment troubled and he frowned a little, but I stared him out until he softly spoke my name and drew me into his arms again.

I wondered whether I could make something up for Trevor so that he felt his questions were worthwhile, but I was too tired.

'Nothing,' I said, 'nothing at all. Can I go back to bed, please?'

Whereas clogged-hair Derrick asks interminably, 'How long are you going to keep this up?'

'Until the end.'

'What do you mean by that?'

What do you think I mean, stupid. Don't you know that passion all ends in death?

'It's like talking to a religious fanatic sometimes, talking to you, Susanna.'

I treat him to an adolescent look of scornful exasperation; an expression which my sister Lin used to dispense to great effect. Privately, however, I conceded that he had made a cogent observation. Probably it is the closest anyone has ever come to understanding. It was the first and only time that I felt respect for Derrick Hearn.

*

In another year it is September again. Olive arrives with the holdall and because it is full of things and I sense she is keen to make gifts of its contents to me I suspect that she will not be coming any more.

Lying on top is a bunch of dahlias, the spiky sort and the ones with petals resembling the paper Christmas decorations which can be concertina'd out, bells, often. 'From the garden,' she says, 'picked this morning.'

When you picked them, could you see the fine raked tilth of the asparagus bed that Jack once worked on, weekend after weekend, so that the skin of his cheeks and the back of his neck were tanned by the sun and the wind? Or is that all long overgrown?

The Pre-Raphaelites are first out of the bag, followed by a sheaf of exhibition catalogues. Then there is a hand-thrown mug with a Tudor rose design worked up in the clay which a potter friend has made. The same friend will provide the wares for the gallery café, apparently. Olive seems fulsomely happy, she radiates warmth like a kitchen range.

Next there is a cake, wrapped in a napkin of some folkweave cloth. She has never said whether the friend with whom she is embarking upon the gallery venture is male or female. Perhaps if it is a male she feels she must observe some nicety towards my father, God help her. Bonnie Jean, asked if she might possibly be able to find a vase for the flowers, returns to praise the baked aroma and is told that it is apple and sultana cake.

A long time afterwards I might be able to acknowledge the irony of the next part of the September afternoon. You see, when my father's wife first walked into this room, I, unable to escape, was filled with fear. I cowered inside my head as I anticipated what she would say and do. Shout, accuse, perhaps strike physical blows, a slap to my deviant, once-painted harlot's cheeks.

Perhaps pelt me with my old clothes, all patterned with that repeat motif of passion spent, and now rags merely. 'Rag and bone' the old man with the horse and cart used to cry through the south London mornings. 'Rag and bone'.

I came to wish that she had done all or any of these things, nothing there to fear. But Olive did none of them; there in the golden perfidious kindness of the September sunshine, what she did do was infinitely worse. My penance was to prove far more subtle.

'There are some old apple trees in the garden,' Tisiphone explains to Bonnie Jean, who will doubtless miss their little chats. 'Marvellous croppers and we always had so many windfalls... so I got into the habit of putting them into a cake, it was my husband's favourite...'

No, it wasn't, you kindly stupid stupidly kind bovine woman who never had children so managed broken adults instead. And even if it was his favourite that was only because he had not yet visited the baker's on the corner of Bywater Street and shared the sweet sandy curranty Nelson cakes with his sweet-mouthed sticky love in the early morning sheets of faraway mist-shrouded Chelsea.

She has cut me a slice but my hand is dead on the cover and so she offers some to Bonnie Jean. All the auxiliaries love to eat whenever they can, always pleased to share in the chocolate box or the toffee tin or whatever is brought in. I think it is the crushing nature of their work and the tedium of it; after all, even madness is boring if you have to see it day in, day out.

And then from the holdall a lumpy carrier bag is taken.

'I'm warning you,' my mother used to say, once, twice or three times before delivering some retributive blow.

'I'll put these in the bowl for you, Susie... they ripen up very well... I'm not sure what the variety is, your father did find out, once upon a time, but I forget...'

Lord Lambourne. And the sun through the glass will ripen them up says Jack while he tries to persuade me that I should leave him and I imagine how it would feel if I did and there is a hole right through the centre of my chest as though someone sculpted my form and cast me in cold bronze for the Chiltern winds to pass through the place where my heart should be.

'Anyway, as it will be the last year I thought I ought to make the most of the old trees. I really think it's the best season we've had... Do try it, Susie...'

Bonnie Jean has declared the cake scrumptious and Olive is telling her that she thinks muscovado rather than caster is the key.

And, 'Aren't you going to eat yours?' they ask me. 'Go on, give it a try...'

'I'm warning you,' my mother said before she laid about her.

And it seems that there is no end to the bounteous harvest from Olive's holdall for she has bobbed down to it yet again.

'Oh, and Susie,' she says, 'I don't suppose you ever remember seeing your father at all and so I thought...' and pauses breathless, '...this I think is my favourite one of him...'

I shut my eyes just in time. If they want to make me look they will have to gouge them open.

'Well, I'll just leave it on the side here then...'

'Take it back. Get it gone. I don't want to see.'

They cluck and whisper at the edge of the room beyond the cinnamon incense of the broken cake. Confetti was little bits of cake thrown by the Romans for nuptial celebrations. I hear a small bump as a stray apple drops from the bowl, one of them replaces it.

'Susie, I can see that you're tired and I have to go soon anyway, but there is one other thing I need to tell you. I've written down the details of the grave, in case you should ever want to go and see... It's in the town where he was born, in Wales.'

'I don't know what you're talking about. He's not dead. I don't know anyone that's dead.'

My eyes are still shut tight.

'Susie, try and listen, it's important to me. Jack, John, your father, was always troubled that because he was away at the war he could not carry out some special wishes his mother had, for her own funeral. He had a little sister, you see, but she died. Her name was Ora. His mother wanted to be buried with Ora but because Jack was away at sea and it was wartime he could not make the arrangements.'

I think this woman is raving mad. My father's body, his long bony el Greco legs cannot be buried in a grave in the ground, wrapped round in a shroud rag. They cannot be weighted down under the dank crow-black earth, those long and energetic legs. And between them his thing, and so often it seemed done and finished like an old flower stalk discarded from the vase. She says Ystradyfwog but I have been to the churchyard in Whitstable where my grandmother was laid; I know that there was a heap where the dead flowers from the graves and the urns were thrown. This heap was beside the place you drew water to fill the urns and in the next field there was the wooden Scout hut and grass where insects buzzed and flicked in the midday heat. Discarded there in their own death mound, petals gone brown and stalks white and limp and fallen over. And yet so easily restored I think, a pinch of sugar in the water, and my father ready once more to beat my sin not out of me but sweetly in again. He cannot be weighted down under dark good night; she makes no sense. Non sense in the things she says.

Mad woman, I am warning you.

'The headstone is rather special. I found an elderly man working locally who had trained with Eric Gill at Capel-y-ffin.'

John ap Rhys Owen lies beside Ora, beloved infant sister.

She is mad. She is trying to make me believe outlandish 'land of my fathers' nonsense. Only non sense can be made out of her District of Ystradyfwog nonsense, sans serif sans sense to say that my father love is in the oblivion of the earth, sans senses, sans eyes, sans taste of me, sans flesh.

I have warned you. What must I do to make you listen, any of you with your sans serif sans sense Gill sans everything nonsense. And before they can make me see or listen to any more of their outlandish non senses I have howled so that the lost mind of the old prize fighter in the next wing will hear and understand and I have hurled the cake at the wall across the room and it hits with the sound of a wet rubber ball thrown in the playground and I have jumped and run from the high bed. In moments I am in the bathroom and I have locked the door and although I know that they will simply unlock it from the other side it will not be before I have sought that third tile up which is three in on the middle row. Such negligence in buildings and works is the beginning of the end at the Springfield Hospital; it signals the new order when us inmates will find the doors unlocked but the world outside cold and only the red plastic warmth of Woolworth's cafeteria in which to huddle away our days.

I take down my cracked tile and its white vitreous edge is as efficient on thirsting flesh as any broken glass or blade.

(O) live has gone. She has been installed in Cornwall for some time now, I think. She sent a
postcard showing the street in which her gallery is sited. In the
foreground was a large gull with yellow stilt legs. After that I did
not hear from her again.

Sister Anna Maria says that it is a pity I am unable to come
out and attend a Mass. She would take me and accept full responsibility, she says, but Herne the Hunter says no. The next best
thing she can do, she feels, is to bring me a copy of the roneo'd
Mass sheet from each Sunday. I can read it at my leisure and I am
to be sure to ask her about anything that I do not understand. I
thank her most sincerely but in private in my head I must admit
that I know enough of the disciplines of Sister Anna Maria's
church to feel guilty that I let her befriend me, even though
I know what I have done and what one day I will be about to
do. There is one sin that I have yet to commit; it follows with a
certain niceness on the other ones. And plenty of torment I have
endured in between times; but no more than I deserved. In any
case, I do not think that Sister Anna Maria is the sort of person
who would wish to rescind her kindness, even when she discov-
ers how truly bad I am.

How shocking I would be to other people if I ever did tell
them the whole truth. I do not shock myself though, I never

have. You see, when my father had me in his embrace, arms and legs and hair all wound around, I used to cling on for dear life in my rapture, thinking only, 'This is what I was made for. This is why I was born.' And everything outside the act of possession was disengaged from me and my clasped love, as the rest of the fairground seems when the merry-go-round is turning.

In the Mass sheets, sometimes smudged, brought by Sister Anna Maria, I liked particularly the passage included in the sheet for the second Sunday of Lent, from St Paul's letter to the Philippians. I think he may have been somewhat weary at the time of writing; he says: *I have told you often, and I repeat it today with tears, there are many who are behaving as the enemies of Christ. They are destined to be lost.*

I asked her whether it was the Rembrandt St Paul and she said that she was not too sure but probably because early on there had been just the one Paul; though subsequently, she adds, you had the Passionist and St Paul Aurelian and so on. Rembrandt's St Paul looks old and weary and ascetic; his head is a bone dome and he seems to be working indefatigably to finish the task in front of him before death claims his entire haggard bag-of-bones old self and stops him. On the death of William Morris the doctor said that the deceased, so unfailingly driven and engaged, died simply of being William Morris. Rembrandt's St Paul looks as though he will go the same way.

Considering that I am deemed insane the volume of facts that I have retained in parts of my memory is quite remarkable. For instance, as well as the major speeches from *Richard II* I still have the streets of Chelsea, squares 5C–5D, 6C–6D, page 76 of the *A–Z of London*, off by heart. I have begun, in finely sharpened fine pencil, to draw myself a map on the end papers of Jack's book on Chagall. Like a maiden lady planning a long journey I pore over my map for hours on end. I have put a cross for the Church of Our Most Holy Redeemer and St Thomas More. If I can get hold of a blue pencil I am going to indicate the plaques for Captain Scott at number 56 and poor Christina Rossetti round the corner on Cheyne Walk.

The river, you know, is not kind. It never has been really. It is a bit of a serpent, winding its wide way.

It is my task to close quite soon. We are back to letter writing again, are we not? Must stop now because... and then I, the writer, might make some cheery cheerio reference to what I am off to do. We know what I am going to do, you and I. I hope that you have understood enough to understand. Jack promised me that it would all be all right but sometimes, I must confess, I have thought that he, slipping easy into his old philanderer's honeyed ways, had lied to me. Now I see that it will be all right, after all. 'Nearly home,' he said to me as arm in arm we retraced hushed Oakley Street on the night that he comforted me on Albert Bridge.

Nearly home. Sometimes these days he is so close to me that I feel the gentle alteration in the air as he leans over my shoulder and tells me to describe what I see in the painting on the page and involuntarily I smile and Bonnie Jean, coming in with the water jug, says she always knew that I would get better.

Last month I was allowed to attend my mother's funeral. It was at the crematorium at Streatham Vale. The chapel there is built of engineering bricks, their surface hard and shiny so that they are never absorbing or softened by the autumn sunlight. I noted that Ron looked much cleaner, now that his hair had turned quite white. My sister's husband and her two meaty boys were attendant upon her in her wheelchair. She had some malfunction of the heart and so they gave her someone else's; she is grotesquely puffed up by steroid treatments.

Before too long Ron and Lin will both be dead. The silent husband, unreconstructed by his expensive suits, will betake himself to Spain. Then, all connections will be cast away. I can return, revenant, to walk through the Chelsea streets on an evening of spring. In Margaretta Terrace the child with the rocking-horse curtains will be long grown and gone to make its fortune. But the camellia may still be there, blooming and dropping its waxy pink petals over the wall to the pavement beneath.

I will carry on until I am outside the Phene Arms. Then I will look up at the room in Oakley Street and I shall see the outline of my father's figure against the window; tall, and the shoulders slightly stooped.